GLITCH

GLITCH

ANIMUS™ BOOK 6

JOSHUA ANDERLE

MICHAEL ANDERLE

DISRUPTIVE IMAGINATION®

LMBPN Publishing
PMB 196, 2540 South Maryland Pkwy
Las Vegas, NV 89109

First US edition, April 2019
ISBN: 978-1-64202-218-6

GLITCH TEAM

Thanks to the JIT Readers

Jeff Eaton
Nicole Emens
John Ashmore
Kelly O'Donnell
Micky Cocker
Misty Roa
Larry Omans

If I've missed anyone, please let me know!

Editor
The Skyhunter Editing Team

*To Family, Friends and
Those Who Love
to Read.
May We All Enjoy Grace
to Live the Life We Are
Called.*

GLITCH

CHAPTER ONE

Seattle's skyline shimmered as the biodome activated. A small pocket formed to release small droplets of rain while a mist swirled and drifted below. Those who walked on the warming spring night welcomed the cooling vapor, their attention focused on the glow of the lights that adorned the Space Needle. These artfully reflected the droplets to swathe the dark sky of the city in an ethereal glow.

Couples walked through the parks and streets while shops closed for the night. Friends wished one another well as they made their way home, while others waited on their companions to come out so they could begin their night.

On the top of the Azure Jewel Condominium building, an odd space of what seemed to be comprised of nothing seemingly broke through the mists as it descended. Of course, no one was aware of this or, even if they had noticed, they would probably have thought little of it.

Perhaps it was because of the way the mist was carried on the wind, or possibly an error on the system that would be repaired in the morning. Enough reasonable explanations could be found when people didn't consciously consider the more bizarre explanation. The drizzle increased to a downpour and drenched the ground and plants below. Umbrellas opened and hoods came up as people shielded themselves from the rain.

The odd spot on top of the Azure Jewel remained unaccountably dry as if the droplets fell onto something above it, caught, and slid off the unseen barrier.

That particular something moved along the roof and vaulted to the edge to look out over the city. The vaguely outline but otherwise invisible figure had grown too impatient to admire the sights.

His target should have been there by now.

Egon Fallon was an incredibly smart man who began his career at Anima technologies and helped in designing EI code. After a decade of service there, he was transferred to a post at the Nexus Academy at Professor Laurie's personal request. He was generally well-mannered and even charming on occasion—although those occasions were rare as he was both a homebody and a workaholic, not the most social of combinations.

His status was of great value to him, one that he had worked hard to obtain. It had gained him entry into some exclusive circles and gave him access to many places within the Academy.

The target was, in fact, perfect for what Gin required.

The revenant looked at the skyline once more. Even with the enhanced sight his visor provided, he couldn't quite make out the dilapidated area he'd called home for a few years while he was on the run and under the guiding hand of his mentor. By now, it was probably another fancy district, catering to the youth or those with creds to part with. Progress had become rather flashy this century.

He should have simply stayed in the condo and waited for the man in relative peace rather than indulge in this sightseeing excursion. But, strangely enough, he felt oddly nostalgic over the place he'd once called home. He wondered, when this was all done, whether he would ever return there. Would he ever come back to Earth, for that matter? He had missed it in the decade-plus he had spent in the great beyond. There were plenty of toys here to amuse him and much variety.

A large holoscreen appeared on the side of a building ahead and caught his attention. News scrolled across it to declare the passing of a beloved celebrity—heart failure, by all accounts. Some things affected the greats as well as the not so greats, apparently.

Gin breathed deeply as he recalled Kilian. In a weird way, to call the man his savior seemed something of an oxymoron considering the profession he'd taught him. He hadn't really given his mentor much thought in a long time, he realized, which meant he probably shouldn't stay where he was. There really were too many bad memories, to say nothing of the Academy.

He thought back to a few of the simulations he'd run and all the missions that had built him up to be something that he could now never be. In all honesty, he didn't have the heart for it.

All those teachers would probably appreciate this—the

first mission he had undertaken in a while, even with Zubanz out of the picture. He would head out to accomplish something with a very specific goal in mind.

In a perverse way, he would make history—the first Nexus student to take on a mission that actually attacked them.

A warning appeared in his visor. His quarry was home. Gin smiled and simply stepped off the edge. The magnetic strips on the soles of his boots clung to the side of the building as he walked down the few stories to greet the man he would be for a while.

Egon finished washing his hair a few seconds before the lights cut out. He sighed as he manually unlatched the shower door, pulled it open, and padded to the bathroom closet for a towel. It had been a while since he'd actually had to use one, so he hoped they weren't musty. A hasty sniff confirmed that this wasn't an issue. He dried himself, wrapped the towel around his waist, and fumbled for his phone on the vanity to contact the management or maintenance department. Someone needed to resolve the problem with the power so he could finish the work he'd planned for the evening.

Something thin and chill snaked around his neck and hoisted him a few inches above the tiles. His phone fell with a clatter, the number undialed. The noose tightened and his legs flailed as his fingers clawed at the constricting cord, but to no avail. His fingers encountered a cold and metallic substance he didn't recognize. Frantically, his bulging eyes peered into the darkness but found no discernible trace of his attacker. Even in the dark, he reasoned, there should be a figure or a shape or even simply a deeper shadow, but his searching gaze found nothing.

He gasped, desperate for breath, and the garotte tightened even more. His desperate attempt to loosen the noose increased as his air passages shrunk to virtually nothing.

"I don't normally do this..." a jovial voice stated. Egon's eyes fluttered as he went limp. A figure emerged slowly from the empty darkness. Energy crackled as an arm, covered in white armor, took shape along with a piece of helmet and a chest plate. On some ridiculously inconsequential level, Egon realized that his assailant most likely used a cloaking generator.

"But trust me, you'd rather die than wait around for this thing to work," Gin said and held the wormwood device up. "Plus, I know how you science types get when you're shown exactly how easily your little inventions can be destroyed—or worse, used for devious purposes."

The technician's vision faded a little but the tension around his throat relaxed to allow him to gasp in a much-needed gulp of air. He managed to focus on the intruder, confusion and panic in his eyes. He wanted to ask who he was—it seemed important to know the name of his killer—but couldn't shape the words. The man hauled him close to his visor. "So consider this my thanks for the DNA."

In one swift motion, he crushed the technician's throat and laid his body on the floor. He knelt beside it and placed the device on the man's chest. It glowed as it activated, and several wires emerged to burrow into the body. A colorless circle appeared and filled gradually with white as the body was drained. While he waited, Gin retrieved Egon's phone, scrolled through, and located a few saved videos—what seemed to be recording things he'd researched outside of Nexus, possibly for personal reasons. Any one of those would provide a suitable voice sample.

The assassin checked the wormwood device. It had almost completed its work. This was, he mused, far more efficient than its original function. He should pay a visit to Liya to see what she'd been up to. When he snapped his fingers a moment later, the power was restored to the room. No one would be any the wiser.

Well, perhaps one person, but the odds were high that he wouldn't tell anyone anything.

The wormwood device finished with a soft hum and the wires retracted from the corpse and curled back. He retrieved it and used his HUD to navigate the options. Once he'd found the voice setting, he played the first file. The device recorded it and bleeped confirmation when it finished.

Gin placed it on Egon's bed, removed his armor, and once he was down to his underlay, stretched out beside his victim. He picked the device up again with a definite grimace. This was where it would get weird—which, for him, meant a level of weird way beyond the average.

He pressed a couple of buttons and placed it cautiously on his chest, then winced as something sharp pierced the skin. A rush of nausea followed, and he steadied himself with a long, deep breath. It certainly felt different to take *on* the life of someone rather than take their life.

Once the discomfort passed, he stood once more and pressed another button on the device. A small chip ejected from the slot on top, which he slid into a compartment on the back of his neck. He waited, a little concerned when nothing seemed to happen immediately. A moment later, he looked at his hands, which were now darker than before. He turned to the mirror and smiled.

He had to admit, Egon did have a nice smile, even if it wouldn't normally have the devious edge it presently did. That, he acknowledged, was something he would have to work on.

Gin exited the bathroom and paused when he saw Egon's faculty card and oculars on the dresser. This would be the first test. He picked the oculars up gingerly and turned them on.

"Good evening, Dr. Fallon," the EI greeted him in a monotone. It was merely a basic skin, a wireframe face with no distinguishable features. His chosen identity seemed to be a man with rather spartan tastes, but the OS certainly signified that this was a professional-grade EI.

"Good evening..." His mind scrolled quickly through the dossier he had compiled for the tech as he tried to remember the EI's name. "Uh...Kaydik, could I ask if anything seems off to you?"

"In what way, Doctor?" Kaydik asked. *"All vitals seem normal. Are you unwell?"*

He smiled smugly. Not even the man's own EI could tell the difference. "Yes, I'm fine—a little exhausted, perhaps, but otherwise fine."

"That is understandable. You've had a long day. I recommend a good night's sleep and a healthy breakfast in the morning. You want to be prepared for whatever tomorrow brings."

Gin nodded, removed the optics, and turned them off. "That sounds perfect."

CHAPTER TWO

The Assault droid's focus was effectively diverted when an explosion shattered the fifth floor of the factory. A large figure used the opportunity to block its view and crush it under a heavy armored foot.

"Get a move on," Luke bellowed as he swung his hammer to clear his path of two other droids. He scowled when a large contingent of the mechanicals issued from the entrance of the factory.

"A bigger group of bots is on the way. They really want us to join the hive mind or something," the titan exclaimed, raised his arm, and activated a shield as the enemy opened fire. He slung his hammer onto his back and readied his hand cannon to return the favor as a laser torrent bore down on him.

"We have more to worry about than a few jobbers." Silas chuckled as he, Marlo, and Raul took position beside him and immediately joined the attack.

"Nice shield." Mack landed in front of the group and

generated a large barrier to block the barrage that threatened the group. "Mine's bigger, though."

"Not bad." Luke chuckled and ventured a few more shots with his hand cannon before he vented it. "How long can you keep it up?"

"None of them have any charged blasters or anything with much punch, but they will probably—wait, was that innuendo?" Mack questioned airily as he fired his hand cannon to good effect against the approaching horde.

"You guys need to back up like Sy said. Soon, the bots won't be the problem here," Kaiden huffed over the comms. Blasts and static discharge could be heard in the background.

"You're still in the building?" Silas asked. The group made a slow retreat toward a hill as the swarm of droids pursued relentlessly. A few of them managed to break through Mack's barrier. "I thought you said you wouldn't be long."

"I have the blueprints and I'm on my way back, but there are way more droids than I thought there would be," the ace responded. More gunfire and muttered curses followed as if to prove his point.

"It's a droid factory," Raul pointed out dryly and fired a few hasty shots at the enemy that broke through the barrier. "There will be a hell of a lot of them."

"Honestly, I thought most of them would be gunning for you after that little stunt," Kaiden admitted.

"Wait, were we bait?" Marlo asked as he released a charged blast from his cannon and obliterated a group of attackers. A few others on the perimeter of the blast were stunned and the surge deactivated them briefly.

"No, you're being helpful," Kaiden countered. "Although you could have been more helpful. A for effort, low B for quality."

"Look out—Havocs!" Mack yelled when a group of about a dozen Havoc droids spilled out of the factory. Dark red eyes glowered at the group as their cannons primed. "My barrier won't last long against those."

"Marlo, you have that upgrade for the cannon, right?" the ace asked above the sound of Sire venting beside him.

"Yeah, but the Havocs look shielded." Marlo looked at the vanguard who nodded. "Yeah, they're shielded, so the normal blasts would be more effective than—"

"I'll take care of that. Get ready, I'll be there in ten." Kaiden went silent before they could argue.

Silas and Raul leapt over the crest of the hill with Luke on their heels. The vanguards remained on the summit. Mack and the trio behind him continued their volleys at the bots while Marlo smacked a switch on the side of his weapon to prime it. The barrel spun and parts inside the muzzle shifted to different areas as an orb of light formed in the chamber. "It's almost ready to go, Kaiden," he shouted into the comms as he raised the cannon.

The Havoc droids immediately launched a concerted barrage that destroyed the shield. Mack stood in front of Marlo and created a concentrated barrier in front of them both, but it was immediately pounded by the havoc droid's blasts and numerous lasers from the others. Some of the smaller mechanicals had run up to the two and now battered on the outside of the barrier.

Luke surged forward down the hill, swept the droids

away with his hammer, and raised his personal shield to extend the defense.

"Step back behind the barrier," Mack instructed, although he struggled to maintain it. "Keep your shield up."

The titan nodded and walked back slowly. When he passed his teammate, his shield immediately disappeared, and its hexagonal pattern merged into the larger barrier. "I added yours to mine," Mack explained. "It strengthens both,"

"You have a few impressive tricks," Luke complimented him. "I don't get to work much with other heavies besides Marlo. The three of us should go on a mission sometime and do some real stomping."

"That sounds great," the vanguard agreed and tried to add another layer to their defense. His efforts were obliterated faster than he could secure them. "Let's try getting this done first, yeah?"

"I feel ya. How are you doing, Marlo?" Luke asked.

The demolitionist propped his cannon up. "I'm ready, but what am I supposed to do, Kaiden? I told you that it—"

"I'll take care of their shields now." He'd no sooner finished his sentence when a large surge of electricity sparked between the massed Havoc droids. It neither damaged nor deactivated them, but their shields were drained, and their fire stopped momentarily.

"Good one," Marlo exclaimed and aimed his cannon. "You two, fall back. This will be a little unruly." Luke and Mack nodded and scrambled behind their large teammate as he fired the weapon. He'd selected a wide beam rather than a blast, which swathed across the droids to either slice through them completely or melt them into twisted chunks of metal. Even the Havoc droids fell, one after another in quick succession, to the infernal ray.

The demolitionist stepped back as the beam weakened and the group covered him as he made his way behind the ridge. Kaiden joined the fray when he sprinted out through the hole in the wall of the factory and onto the battlefield.

The cannon finally lost its charge, and Marlo ducked out of sight behind the ridge and vented the massive weapon, turning it onto its side so he could open the core. "I'm done for now. That beam is powerful, but it overheats the core badly," he explained. "I still have my hand cannon, but the big gun will be out for a while."

"More are incoming," Raul warned. "Kaiden, get over here. You're in the way of my shots."

"Thanks for the concern," the ace muttered sarcastically and unleashed a charged shot at a trio of Guardian droids before he sprinted to the group. "Mack, I'll have Chief send you an algorithm. Can you make a shield using it?"

The details appeared on the vanguard's HUD. "Uh... Yeah, not a problem, but this won't block anything but— oh..." Mack turned to the group. "Everyone, get down."

"What are you doing, Kaiden?" Silas demanded as the ace slid down the hill and stopped beside him.

"Something Genos taught me," he stated cryptically as the vanguard created a dark-blue barrier around them.

"It's ready, Kaiden." He nodded to reinforce his words.

"Good. Hit it, Chief," Kaiden ordered. A large blast spewed a wave of white energy that passed over the shield. Loud cracks and pounding noises followed before it went silent.

"What was that?" Marlo asked as the shield deactivated.

"EMP. The factory was comprised of numerous smaller cores instead of one larger one, so I used a couple of them to set it off," he explained and checked his weapon. "The shield I had Mack set up should have prevented it from messing with our equipment. Our heavies are all still standing instead of toppling from the weight of their armor, so that's a good sign."

"You know how to do that?" Silas asked incredulously.

"Not really. Genos does, though. He's given me pointers from time to time and still had to walk me through it." he admitted and placed a hand on the side of his helmet. "Speaking of which, I should probably check in with the other teams before the big guy arrives. How are you doing, team B?"

"We're in the hanger," Jaxon answered. "We should arrive shortly unless team C was able to finish faster than we hoped."

"I haven't heard from them yet, but I don't see the Colossus yet—" Rumbles and rending sounds in the distance could only signify destruction. The group peered over the summit and froze at the sight of the massive, bipedal machine that now stalked toward them, crushing trees underfoot. "Well, shit."

"That thing is huge, even from this distance," Luke shouted and looked disconsolately at his hammer. "Maybe I could crush a toe?"

"If you wanna take a run at that thing, be my guest," Raul muttered and stowed his rifle. "I, for one, will simply leg it in the other direction. It might be far away now, but it covers more ground in a step than we can in a full sprint. Distance is our only advantage."

"I'm not that worried about it trampling us." Kaiden took a few steps back as he pointed to the giant droid. "I'm more worried about those big-ass guns."

As if to prove his point, the mechanical raised an arm, its hand replaced by an enormous cannon that aimed unerringly at the group.

"Well, it's been fun, guys." Silas sighed but was immediately shoved by both Kaiden and Raul.

"Scatter," the ace ordered. The group broke off in different directions as the Colossus charged its weapon.

"Team C, we request help if you can," Kaiden called over the comm link. He froze at a massive rush of air and glanced back. A massive orb glowed in the threatening cannon. "Now would be good."

"We're still working on it, Kaiden," Izzy responded. "Genos and I have almost reached the core, but it's been tricky. There is substantial reinforcement in the area around the core and trying not to die from the radiation has also been a concern."

"Can you shut the cannon down or something? The other thing can wait," he demanded.

"We only have partial control of the systems, Kaiden," Chiyo explained. "Even with Otto and I working together, we can only access it for a few moments before control is ripped away. The security in this machine's systems is incredible."

"I'm glad you've found something that challenges your interest," Kaiden huffed. "But if I could make a slight request, I would prefer not to feel what it's like to be ripped apart atom by atom. I find even the thought definitely uninteresting."

"I'm in, but only for movement," Otto interjected. "Let me try something."

The ace glanced back as the dark sky illuminated, the energy of the Colossus' cannon almost like an artificial sun. He braced himself, but the robot moved its arm fractionally upward as it fired. The orb careened overhead to land more than a mile away, but the force still hurled him, Silas, and Raul back. Kaiden collided painfully with a tree and lost sight of his companions, temporarily blinded by the blast.

"Are you still alive?" Otto asked tentatively.

The unnatural glow of the charge had dimmed and only a few hundred yards away, a crater had been gouged by the blast. "Yeah, by barely a couple of football fields. What did you do?"

"I changed the direction slightly. It was the only option," he explained. "Chiyo and I are doing everything we can to stall this thing, but like she said, the security system is a real pain."

"And yet she makes it sound like it's fun." Kaiden stood and shook the dust off, then froze at the sound of slipstream engines above.

"Are you guys trying to kill us? Cameron demanded over the comms. The ace squinted at the three fighter ships that rocketed over him and toward the Colossus.

"It's good to see you guys finally pulling your weight," he joked. "Only three ships? Weren't there five of you?"

"Amber's in here with me," Flynn stated. The ships on the left and right banked to either side to surround the giant mech before they opened fire. "Julius is with Jaxon. He said Cam seemed ornery."

"We trekked through miles of jungle, took on a squad of mercs, and are now laying siege to a big-ass robot with three small fighters," Cameron retorted. "I think I've earned the chance to— Shit, look out!"

Dozens of small compartments opened on the mech to reveal turrets that fired immediately. All three aircraft took evasive maneuvers to avoid the barrage as the enemy continued to advance.

"How are you doing, Genos?" Kaiden asked fretfully as Silas limped over to him.

"I've reached the central chamber and sent Izzy to disconnect a few couplings while I try to deactivate the back-up. If it works, it should deactivate the machine," the Tsuna explained.

"And if it doesn't?"

"It would still momentarily power down but would reactivate and probably send a surge of energy through the body that would fry all four of us." He sounded both calm and unbelievably cheerful.

Silas placed a finger on his helmet. "You'd better not mess this up, Izzy," he warned.

"Build me up here, Sy," she grunted as she yanked a coupling apart.

"I'm hit," Flynn called. "Ejecting!"

"We need to get over there," Kaiden stated.

"And do what exactly?" Silas asked and frowned as he looked around "Where the hell did Raul go?"

"According to the map, somewhere that way." The ace pointed into the distance as he increased his pace. "If Flynn and Amber make it to the ground, they'll need cover."

"So what? We annoy it?"

He shrugged. "Or be bait."

"Great." Silas clicked his tongue dismissively but jogged beside his teammate. The three heavy fighters were already on the field and tried to destroy a few of the turrets. Their efforts only made the guns swing around and fire upon them. Flynn and Amber crash-landed in small pods and Kaiden and Silas each ran up to one to help the occupants out.

"Are you all right?" Kaiden asked Flynn.

"I can't believe Cameron outlasted me." The marksman sighed and his quick glance studied the Colossus. "That's a big beasty."

"You're right." The ace nodded but a shadow fell over the party to quell a light-hearted response. The truth was a little more sobering. "And it's also about to step on us."

"That's a damn shame," Flynn said nonchalantly.

The group once again braced for death but for some reason, their enemy stopped in mid-motion. Everyone used the opportunity to race out of its path.

"Was that you, Chiyo?" Kaiden asked.

"Indeed. The system becomes easier to bypass as Genos and Izzy disrupt the machine's power source. Most of the tasks seem to focus on sustaining the Colossus."

"I shall be finished momentarily," Genos interjected. "Those of you within the machine might wish to hold on to something in case of impact or potential disintegration."

The mechanical's turrets stopped firing and the gargantuan foot descended a few paces from the group. For a moment, it twitched and sputtered as if it battled against some sort of restriction before it went still.

The group exchanged glances and studied their adversary cautiously.

"Well, we're not getting shot at anymore so that's an improvement," Cameron stated. "Is anyone dead?"

"We're all good down here." Luke looked at Kaiden, his expression seeking confirmation.

"What about y'all inside?" the ace asked. The only response was dead air.

For a moment, he worried that the Colossus would reactivate, but Flynn tapped him on the shoulder and pointed at the mech's shoulder. He zoomed in with his visor and smiled when he saw Genos scramble out and help Izzy do the same.

"Kaiden, are you there?" Chiyo asked, her voice slivered with static.

"I am," he replied with a broad grin as a banner scrolled across his visor. **Mission complete.**

"Good job on not dying," he said with a smile.

"Same to you." He heard her laugh as she signed off and they were desynced.

CHAPTER THREE

Laurie took the final sip of wine and sighed as he handed the glass to one of the door guards, waved his hand to dismiss him, and drew a deep breath. He placed his hand against the scanner. After an affirmative green light flashed above the door, it opened, and he entered reluctantly. This was the third meeting he'd had with the board this month—three times more than he usually tried to have in a year. Never was his real preference, of course, but even he understood necessary evils.

Unfortunately, he was an expert in those too.

He crossed the corridor and the final door opened, and he walked into the board room. Sasha awaited him and gestured for him to take the seat beside him. The professor linked his hands on the table and faced the other members of the board—Victoria, Oswald, Vincent, and Olivia.

"It's good to see you've finally returned, Vincent," he muttered and fixed the board member in question with a challenging look. "Did you have fun meeting with the council?"

"Of course. Being able to interact with a group of right-minded people who have a noble cause was a pleasant experience," Vincent retorted and earned a glare from Laurie as well as a sideways glance from Oswald and Olivia.

Sasha adjusted his oculars and cleared his throat. "Let's not start this off on such a sour note." He looked at both Vincent and Laurie. "This is hopefully the conclusion to the talks about project Orson. We've brought up the complications and new findings, along with the fact that some of the students seem to be suspicious as to what is going on."

"It shouldn't have gotten to this point in the first place," Laurie snapped. "When we originally developed this idea, it was agreed that it would only be in very specific, controlled situations." The professor, in a surprising show of anger for him, slammed his fist on the table and pointed to Vincent. "Until you decided that it should be used for actual missions. Why? Merely to please the council? At this point, why do you even stay here? Go off and be their lackey. I'm sure they could find a use for you, whether it's lobbying for them or simply on your knees."

"Shut your mouth, Laurie," Vincent responded, his tone heated. "You've known about the changes to the project. I might have initially omitted to mention that things had progressed down a different path, but you knew full well where it would lead. And don't pretend that you never discovered it until now. Maybe your sudden anger at the situation is simply because it now involves your little pet project?"

"Back down, both of you," Oswald snapped. "To think that men of such stature could bark like rabid dogs—"

"While I agree that the professor and the director should both deescalate the situation, I have to say that I understand Laurie's frustrations," Sasha intervened.

"Of course you do," Vincent spat. "But siding with one of your friends shows bias in these matters, doesn't it?" The director's cold eyes challenged the commander. "Besides, you have your own stake in Laurie's experiment. You were the one who brought him here in the first place, weren't you?"

"I did, but that is not the concern," Sasha retorted equably and ignored the other man's insinuation. "As we've discussed in the previous meetings, we have gone too far with the plan. It's becoming troublesome and a risk to both students and the reputation of this Academy. We were already in murky waters when we agreed to this, but we expected it to further our causes at little to no risk. As of these last few months, that has escalated to a point where we can no longer control it and the consequences can not only be disastrous but also put our students in serious danger."

"That's why we use the homunculi soldiers," Victoria interjected. "No one is at risk during these missions, and the bodies degrade and waste away when completed, leaving no trace. There are no repercussions with this project."

"It also increases the damage to the students' bodies," Laurie countered. "You would have to be blind not to see the stress and fatigue on most of the subjects. Maybe you don't leave your office much, Victoria, but trust me when I say I have enough information and physical evidence to show that there are 'repercussions' with this. The way the Animus connects the students' minds to the homunculi only increases the connection—and, therefore, the pain and blowback when they are injured. They might not come back with physical wounds, but the mind can only take so much stimulation before it affects them. This could lead to a risk of mental breakdowns or potential calamities like strokes or heart attacks."

"Is that any better than one of them leaving this Academy only to get a laser through their head? Or a blade in their throat?" she countered. "Despite your altruistic straw-manning, you know why we began this project."

"I know why I worked on it, which was what was said before we began it," Laurie reminded them. "That this could lead to something that could spare us lives in future wars. But that won't do us much good if all those potential soldiers die before they even graduate."

"I understand your concern, professor," Olivia began. "But you overstate things. As you said yourself, no one has died or gone insane. The current issues are purely physical."

"You say that so calmly," Laurie murmured and shook his head. "What'll it take for you to understand? For someone to finally break?"

"None of us want that," Oswald interjected in a very obvious attempt to placate him. "The students in the Academy are under our protection while they remain here, but can you blame us for wanting this to succeed?"

"The professor is well aware of the potential boons of this project." Sasha waved Laurie's protest aside. "But what concerns him and me is that you seem to allow those potential boons to blind you to the very real dangers. Of the twenty-seven trials, most ended in the students being sent to the med bay for a day of rest." He activated a small EI device to display several graphs. "These are readouts of all the students' physical conditions after desyncing. Eighty-nine percent of them came back exhausted and complained about phantom pains in various areas where they were damaged, although no physical wounds were found. Internally, there were signs of stress as if the body was reactive to moderate to severe injury."

"That is concerning," Olivia said after she'd studied the charts for a moment. "But what about the ones who did not?"

"There are six. Interestingly enough, four of them are technicians, one a soldier, and one Tsuna engineer. They do show higher than average fatigue, but not the same issues as the others."

"That soldier is the one you look after," Victor reminded Laurie. "Could that special EI of his be the reason he has been able to keep up thus far?"

"I wouldn't doubt it." The professor folded his arms and leaned back. "But I've told you before that Kaiden's EI is unique and that he can only use it due to biological happenstance. Unless you're secretly working on a project to mutate DNA—which, I should remind you, has been done before with disastrous results—I would shelve whatever thoughts are bubbling in your head."

"So you're saying that our best bet is with him, then?" Victoria asked.

Laurie looked at Sasha, his displeasure evident, but a

hint of concern crept onto his face. The commander leaned forward and fixed the vice-chancellor with a hard look. "You seem to be leading into something. Speak out."

"Between our previous conversations and hearing the professor's impassioned voice, I'm inclined to agree that perhaps we have done as much as we can here. Or, at the very least, as much as we should do." Vincent turned and glared at Victoria, but she held her hand up. "But I think we should perform one last test,"

"After all this, you still want to—" Laurie shouted and gritted his teeth, but Sasha placed a hand hastily on his shoulder to silence him and pulled him back to his seat.

"Would you care to explain your stance, Vice-Chancellor?" Sasha prodded.

"This project began at the behest of the council, as Laurie reminded us. Terminating the project now may be possible, but if we can show them the full capabilities, they might be more inclined to continue the project themselves. This would leave us in an advantageous position as we would have accomplished something for them and earned their good graces, as well as leave the door open for potential connections in the future."

"You want to continue this dance with the devil?" Laurie snarked. "Why did we even bother to leave the WC if you're so inclined to continue working with them?"

"Because it's easier to get things done with their backing," she responded. "On top of that. if they take on the project proper, any concerns you have with this getting out are reduced as they would be the ones to shoulder the scrutiny."

"Or praise." Oswald chuckled. "But that's how things work with the government, isn't it?"

"It seems like a possibility." Sasha nodded and Laurie glared at him with shocked eyes. "But from your statement before, I assume you have a particular person in mind?"

"Of course." Victoria nodded. "He's the one who's best suited to handle it, as per your stats and his EI advantage—the ace Kaiden Jericho."

"We can't let this go through, Sasha," Laurie exclaimed as the two of them left the board room. "Kaiden is the one who is suspicious. We decided to pull the plug in the first place because of him."

"I'm not happy, Laurie," the commander said in a low tone, his voice almost a whisper. "Not with this decision and not with the fact that I turned a blind eye to it in the first place. But in the circumstances, this was the best I could hope for considering that no one in that room besides the two of us wants this project put on ice."

"What about the chancellor?" Laurie asked as they made their way out of the corridor. "He should have the final say in the fact that we—"

"Durand has already washed his hands of this." Sasha sighed. "I don't blame him. He tried to cancel this project when Vincent and the others moved forward originally, and he's under more scrutiny than the rest of us. But, now that we have a plan, we can focus on finishing this and Durand will be useful to keep the council placated until then."

They exited the building in a tense silence. Laurie strode to the edge of the island and his companion followed after a moment, curious as to what the professor would do. The man simply stepped up to the railing, rested his hands on it, and looked out at the sea and moon. He was silent for almost a minute before he exhaled a deep breath. "I should have done more before it ever got to this point." He grimaced. "I let the fact that I hate dealing with those clowns stop me from sharing my thoughts. I suppose I also got wrapped up in the potential of the project."

"It was a good idea, Laurie," Sasha reassured him with a hand on his shoulder. "It still is, but we overreached our grasp in this situation. All we can do now is fix it and hand it off. And keep the students safe from now on."

"At Kaiden's expense?" Laurie turned to face the commander. "He might be the best one to handle this, but I think that—" His train of thought ceased abruptly, and a small smile formed on his lips. "That snarky bastard has made me worry about him. When I first met him, I thought he would be such a pain."

"I still believe he is," Sasha pointed out dryly and met the other man's gaze with a soft smile. "But I suppose that is, in part, the reason he is endearing."

The professor scoffed, followed by a quick laugh before he turned away and gazed at the moon once again. "Should we tell him?" he asked.

Sasha was silent for a long while as he through it over. "Someday, we'll have to."

CHAPTER FOUR

The executive looked out the window of his mansion that boasted a clear view over the city of Rome. In the distance, he could see the Colosseum—or, rather, the holographic interpretation of it since most of the ancient structure had been destroyed during the Aston wars.

Humanity, in all its glory, has made more than its share of mistakes, that one included.

He turned at a knock at his door and sat at his desk before he called for his visitor to enter. Cole Wilhelm complied and crossed the room quickly. "Have you seen the news?" he asked, worry evident in his voice.

"Concerning what, exactly?" the man asked. "You know that I'm to be kept in the loop about a multitude of things."

"We think we found Gin Sonny in Seattle," Cole explained and handed him a tablet. "We're not sure what he's looking for, but he was seen around one of the highrise districts—or, at least, we picked up a signature that matched the emissions of his suit,"

"If I had to take a guess, he's looking for someone useful." The executive pondered the possibilities as he scrolled through the tablet. "Or, perhaps, simply someone's face that's useful. It's not much of a concern for us."

"Sir, if it gets out that we—"

"Hired him? *We* did no such thing," he said firmly, retrieved a vape pen from his drawer, and took a quick drag. "One of our partners did, and if it is ever discovered, we will disown them and make a show of support in stopping him—if he's still on the planet by that point."

Cole looked at his superior with confusion like he tried to understand the implication before he was forced to ask for clarity. "There's a chance that he'll still head to the Academy. I would say that's almost a definite considering that he's still in the area."

"If that is him in the first place," the man said nonchalantly. "By the way, delete these files when you have a chance." He handed the tablet back. "There's no need to leave a trail that'll implicate us."

"Are you sure we should do nothing, sir?"

The executive took another long drag and smiled with cold humor. "We never do nothing, Cole. We're always at work for the mission. In this case—if Gin is heading to the Academy—no matter what he does, it is a boon for us. Even if he fails, they will grow paranoid. Then, I and my fellow members will act as a face for the World Council and offer our aid, allowing us to gain more access to the Academy. And should he succeed? Well, then…" He smiled and looked at a small hologram on his desk of an EI in the shape of an orb that glowed with a golden light. "We'll have a body to recover."

Kaiden entered the auditorium with the dozens of other students, all prepared to hear what their second-year finals would be. Several teachers and faculty members had already gathered on the stage, but no one he was familiar with. It seemed that Sasha didn't feel like popping in this time around.

He waved at Jaxon and Genos in the Tsuna row, who waved in return as they took their seats. Genos wore new oculars, so he must have been given an upgrade. The Tsuna were a few rows deeper this year, which suggested that the integration plan was working out if they trusted them with more students.

Chiyo and the others were upstairs and seemed to have secured the front row of seats. The ace nodded and greeted them as he walked over to Chiyo, wiggled his fingers at her, and smiled.

"It's good to see you, Kaiden." She greeted him cheerfully as he slid into the seat beside her. "Did you rest well?"

He stretched out and kicked his feet up to rest them on the railing in front of him as the others took their seats along the row. "I'm rather dandy, actually. I hope it was enough rest, though. I'm due to see Wolfson later."

"It's been quite some time since the two of you have gotten together, hasn't it?" she inquired.

"A few weeks. I'm sure he'll put me through the wringer." He grimaced as he imagined the potential beating he might receive. "Although it's not all on me. I tried getting together with him a couple of weeks back, but he was preparing for another visit with Raza. He'll come by soon."

"I'll have to properly introduce myself this time," Chiyo commented. "I don't normally have the chance to meet a Sauren."

"It's one hell of an experience, especially if you fight one," Kaiden said and recalled Wolfson and Raza's little test immediately before the Death Match. "What about you? Didn't you tell me you did some more work with Laurie's personal assistants after the mission yesterday—the ones you worked with over the summer?"

"Yes, Cyra and Raynor. They are both infiltrators, not assistants."

"That's kinda splitting hairs, ain't it?"

"In the same way that you prefer to be called a professional instead of merely a merc," she countered.

"Touché," Kaiden acknowledged. "What about Laurie? Did you hear anything about him?"

She nodded. "They told me to let you know that he would like you to come by whenever it's convenient."

The ace frowned. "That might be the most casual he's been when it comes to requesting my presence. I wonder what the board has done to him. He mentioned that he's had more talks with them than he'd like."

"They said that he did speak about you but that it was more about things surrounding you and didn't elaborate on what that meant."

"Well, that's weird," Kaiden said thoughtfully with a small scowl as he considered the possibilities. "I know weird is kinda his thing, but he's usually not so cryptic."

"He has always seemed rather enthralled with you. Perhaps it's a new project or device he wants you to try out," she suggested.

"That's a possibility. Then again, maybe that could end up with me having more things stuck inside me," he grumbled. "Still, I suppose I wouldn't mind some new toys to play with if that is what he's working on." He looked at Chiyo. "I don't say this often, but enough about me. What did you work on this time? More hush-hush things that you had to take a vow of secrecy to work on?"

"Nothing like that. It was mostly me and Cyra. She helped me work on different exercises and passed on a list of maps and scenarios that she used to run when she was a student here. They look extremely helpful."

"Maps that would prove a challenge even to you?" the ace inquired skeptically.

"There is always room to grow and more to learn, particularly with how fast security adapts and programming changes. I'm happy to learn from those who have already proven themselves, especially if they work directly with the creator of the Animus."

Kaiden was genuinely impressed and wanted to ask what exactly she'd learned and how they could use it in missions. Before he could, the lights above dimmed, and the stage was illuminated. Holoscreens activated on the front of the balcony, and Chancellor Durand's smiling face appeared in them. The ace peered through the translucent screens and confirmed that the chancellor had taken the podium on the stage.

"Good morning, students—or should I say, advas?" he

greeted, his tone crisp and business-like. "We are fast approaching the end of your second year. You have fought hard, learned much, and have paved your own road over this long year. Now, it is time to continue that determination and climb once more."

"You know, at first, I found these speeches inspiring. Now, I wonder if he's reading off cue cards," Kaiden snarked but Chiyo stared at him with a no-nonsense look and a finger on her lips.

"You are now upperclassmen and have students who look up to you and follow your example. I believe you have all risen to that challenge very well, for the most part. But in the next year, you will deal with greater trials as you claim the title of master—not a title to be taken lightly, and one that you will have to earn using the accumulated knowledge and training you have thus far. This, of course, begins with your upcoming final." He looked at the crowd with a smile. "Which, I would guess, is the reason most of you look so anxious."

Some of the students proclaimed agreement loudly. Durand nodded and raised a hand to quiet them as he continued. "This Academy has earned its elite reputation for the kind of men and women we raise, and if you were to balk or leave in fear, I doubt you would have been here, to begin with." His face turned solemn for a moment before it relaxed again as quickly. "Which leads me to discuss your finals for this year. In the spirit of the title of master, you will show that you are indeed on your way to mastering your class. As such, the finals will be a 'throwback' of sorts." The chancellor looked around the auditorium, his audience now utterly silent. "Your tests will be done solo, and your victory is in your hands alone."

The face on the holoscreens faded away to make way for the profiles of the various students that scrolled continuously.

"Unfortunately, not all three-hundred students made it to the end of this year, but the two hundred and eighty-two of you who are still here have earned your place. The sand is always shifting, however, and I hope all of you know when it's time to move to stable ground."

"What's he on about?" Flynn wondered aloud.

Kaiden glanced at him and shrugged. "I haven't the foggiest notion. He's probably trying to build up some mystique."

"It's rather odd that we've gone back to solo tests considering that all the tests this year has been team-based," Silas noted.

"I suppose that just as team skills are important, they can also lead to over-reliance," Chiyo reasoned. "This is a way to show that we haven't forgotten our personal training."

"You should leave this theater and immediately head to the Animus Center and the training grounds, search through tablets in the library, and do everything you can to prepare yourselves for this test," the chancellor stated, fierce determination in his eyes. "You have one week. What happens between then and now is up to you. But you have all proven yourselves thus far and all those on this stage and in this school believe that you will continue to do so. You are Nexus students. You have earned that distinction, but it will only mean something once you graduate and we know that both you and I have done our jobs."

As the crowd began to chatter and shout approvingly in response, the holoscreens disappeared. Kaiden removed his legs from the railing and leaned over for a closer look at Durand, who stood confidently in the center of the stage. "Prepare yourselves, future masters. Bring those talents to the forefront and claim your success."

CHAPTER FIVE

"Hey, Egon, how's it going?" an advisor said in greeting, and her face was scanned quickly for instant identification. **Advisor Faraji.**

"I am doing well, thank you, advisor," Egon stated pleasantly as he passed her. She turned and caught up to walk side by side with him down the hall, a smile on her face.

"So, what brings you to the AC?" she asked pleasantly. "We don't see you here often. Are we getting a new update?"

"Sometime soon, perhaps," he responded and gave her a casual glance. "Right now, I'm simply taking a look around. I don't spend as much time here as I should. I need to make sure I remember my old stomping grounds."

"Well, it's nice of you to drop by," she stated. "If you have any free time later, I'd love to pick your brain—metaphorically, of course. It would probably take hours if I wanted to go through it and check every nook and cranny."

Egon permitted himself a small chuckle at the bizarre joke. "You flatter me, Advisor."

"You can call me Akello, Egon. We're not so formal around here." She paused at one of the Animus pod halls. "I have to set up for the day, but it was nice to see you."

"Likewise. Have a pleasant day."

She waved casually and as she turned away, he heard her whisper, "I made him giggle."

Man, this Egon guy must have been a real downer, the killer thought. Maybe he'd actually done them all a favor by taking his place.

He grinned and continued to the mainframe.

Gin held his stolen security chip to the mainframe's entrance. As it opened, he waved his hand and activated the blackout—his pet name for the mod Vinci had created —to be sure to strike his name from the list of people who accessed the area and hide him from the cameras and sensors in the room. He had to be careful, though. If he taxed it too much, he could overload it or worse, and now would not be a good time for that.

He entered a large room that contained dozens if not hundreds of terminals and servers. Wire and cables daisy-chained between them and the low overhead lighting above was offset only by the multitudes of lights that glowed from the equipment itself.

Even with his mission in mind, he took a moment to look around in awe at the sight. This was the heart of the Animus.

And, he reminded himself smugly, it would lead him directly into the mind of Kaiden Jericho.

His focus restored, he wandered down the corridor between servers and monitors. These were connected to particular halls or had distinct functions related to the process, and as much as he liked to be thorough, they were too specific for what he needed.

Rather than allow himself to be distracted by the possibilities they presented, he made steadfastly to the end and the central station. He smiled, having reached his real destination.

"Dr. Fallon, might I ask what we are doing here?" Egon's EI asked.

"A personal job, Kaydik." Gin answered in the professor's low-toned voice, although with considerably more mirth than was typical for the man. "I intend to put on a show for this Academy."

"Doing anything to the central station is inadvisable, Doctor," Kaydik warned. *"Even minor changes could have disastrous consequences, and you have also not advised other technicians of your plans. I believe we should consult with Professor Laurie before you do anything that—"*

The killer removed the oculars and traced his finger along them to activate blackout. Using the HUD in his personal ocular contacts, he reconfigured the EI before he replaced the oculars.

"How can I be of service, Gin?" it asked, the tone neutral and the life-like inflections normal for EIs now stripped away.

"For now, sit pretty," he ordered as he retrieved the

BREW device from his coat pocket. "I'll take care of everything."

He examined the console, looking for an outlet in which to insert the device before he smacked his own head with real irritation. "Duh," he muttered, pressed the switch on top of the tech, and placed it on the panel.

The BREW device immediately connected to Gin's oculars. He looked at the mainframe and selected it as the target, and the device set to work.

It truly was amazing, he thought proudly—like an infiltrator in a bauble and a very, very good infiltrator at that. The monitor on the central station came to life and screens and panels flashed quickly as the BREW device made its way into the system. What could have taken him hours with the extremely high risk of discovery was literally completed in seconds.

The screen froze to display a multitude of options. Gin smiled in anticipation. "Open directory," he ordered, and another panel dropped down. "Search for Kaiden Jericho."

In a couple of seconds, the student's personnel file and Animus clearance flashed on the screen, and the killer's smile widened. It was time for the BREW device to fulfill its real purpose.

"Activate the revenant virus," he stated with a theatrical snap of his fingers. He had already prepared it, so that should reduce the time necessary for it to upload. The infiltration device would take care of all the incidentals and hiccups.

He scowled when a red warning sign appeared in his HUD and for a moment, he wondered if he'd overestimated the tech's efficiency. It did seem too good to be true.

More than a little disgruntled, he studied the message to discover that it was less of a warning and more of a troubleshooting guide. The short version was that the virus couldn't be uploaded without properly syncing with the intended target, blah, blah, blah…it would need integration with specific parameters…uh huh…synchro variable? What the hell?

Gin read the specifics once again and reasoned through each line. Essentially, the problem seemed to come down to the fact that it required a connection with the target—one that would require time to develop and for Kaiden to remain in the Animus for a while so that it could target him specifically. Otherwise, the virus would simply disrupt the entire system and do squat but get him found out and maybe shut the Animus system down for a while.

There were other options, he decided as he stroked his chin and considered them. One was that he was already in the Academy so he could simply stab him and be done with it.

"Gin is… Because of you, he is…"

Placido's voice resonated in some quiet space within, sad and desperate but full of rage. It floated in his mind and clawed at the memories so long hidden. He tried to shake it loose and force the memories to disappear, but more seemed to flow through that single hazy crack in his stone-hard control.

…he felt a warmth in him at the kindness the ace had displayed as the area turned white and they were de-synced.

The killer looked up and around at the mainframe as if to find something on which to anchor his wayward emotions. The awe he'd felt earlier was slowly replaced by anger as more memories swirled. He focused on the console once more and homed in on the BREW device. This wasn't only about Kaiden—not anymore.

He wanted to show them that they were not safe there, that this wasn't the Nexus that showed the world the best it could be. This was the Nexus that couldn't keep its students safe—the Nexus that had created *him*.

"Copy Kaiden Jericho's ID number and Animus access code," he instructed, and his little miracle tech complied immediately. "Set those as your target. It'll be piece by piece, but you'll have your connection."

The display flashed again as Kaiden's picture came on screen. He studied it and wondered at the parallels. The student was about Gin's age when he'd left, and both were no stranger to violence at that age in their lives. He took a few steps back as he continued his scrutiny of the image. *Fate can certainly be a bitch, can't it, Kaiden?* He had always known he would come back one day and had he promised himself that a few times over the years. Now, there he was, originally at the behest of someone else but there all the same.

On some level, Gin wondered if he would have even considered a plan like this without everything that had happened. Probably not, but it was no real fault of his own. It merely wasn't his style. But now that the opportunity with all its delicious possibilities was in his grasp, what would happen would be much worse than simply coming back and causing a little violence. He intended to shake this Academy down to its very foundation, albeit more metaphorically than literally.

After all, what was the point of coming to Nexus for the Animus if the Animus was its own breed of nightmare?

Another notification flashed on the screen to confirm that everything was in place and instructing him to install the BREW device.

He allowed himself one last look at Kaiden's face before he turned the knob on the small piece of tech. Carefully, he placed it on the rear of the console and the wires unfurled to attach itself securely. A bright white light glowed for a moment before it changed to green and finally, red.

The trap was in place and now, it simply needed the bait. That, he thought smugly, would come soon.

As Gin left the mainframe, he turned at the door and activated blackout once again to remove any possible trace that he had been there.

In time, of course, they would certainly know. It would merely be too late.

CHAPTER SIX

The ace flung himself aside as Wolfson barreled forward, then immediately spun to fire another force shot from the hand-cannon. It struck the giant in the arm and the man stumbled sideways. He recovered well, however, and whirled as he snatched a bola from his belt and threw it with lethal aim. The soldier fired instinctively, and the force of the blast hurtled it back to swipe it past Wolfson's head.

"So, did you miss me after all this time?" Kaiden asked with a bemused grin. "I guess so—you brought the launcher out again. It's been weeks."

The head officer scoffed, raised his weapon, and fired two impact grenades. The ace ducked behind one of the compact walls on the training floor a split second before the ordnance detonated and created a wave of force behind the barrier. Kaiden peeked over cautiously and fired another force shot. It impacted the man squarely in his chest, although it seemed to do less damage than the injury to the arm.

"You chose a really crappy weapon," Chief chided.

"They are all practice weapons, so it's not like the heat or shock weapons would be any better," he countered. "Besides, it's not like he's done much better—*Jesus!*" He jerked back as a dumbbell rocketed past. "Are you trying to kill me?"

"Pay attention, idiot," Wolfson retorted. "You don't come around for a few weeks and suddenly, you've fallen back on all your bad habits. Knock the rust off, boyo."

"I'd rather knock you off, you stupid, gigantic, beard-head," he shouted with spite and vigor as he charged.

"Excellent playground taunting. Now, fight on par with that and we might make some progress."

"Good of you to give me a warning beforehand—really generous of you," his adversary scoffed as he aimed his launcher downward and fired another impact round at the floor directly in front of Kaiden. It went off and knocked the soldier back. "I guess I'll share something in exchange. I only have a few shots left." The giant opened the launcher and retrieved four grenades from his pouch. "And when I'm done with these, should you survive, I'll come for you personally."

"For the love of God, I hope it's not a bear hug."

Wolfson took aim with his launcher in a desultory fashion.

"Stop blathering and show me what else you have. I'll take you down today," the ace retorted acidly.

"Puff your out chest a little more. That'll really sell it," Chief suggested sarcastically.

"Come on, big guy. Are you simply gonna stare at me with a face only a fist could love?" He jabbed his fist in mock punches to make his point. "I'd be happy to oblige if you're lookin' for a little—"

"*Uh—he looks pissed off,*" the EI pointed out as the head officer quietly loaded his launcher with his remaining rounds. "*Granted, that could be the normal Wolfson resting face, but you might wanna hoof it.*"

"Let's see what he has," he proclaimed boldly as he aimed his hand cannon at his opponent, who did the same.

"*Why are you so calm about this?*" Chief protested.

"Firing!" Wolfson shouted and immediately dispatched three rounds. His target was able to knock two out of the air, but one whizzed past his head. Kaiden gained a cocky grin, but the giant merely grinned in response and pointed behind him. The ace whirled as the grenade bounced off a pillar and boomeranged back to him.

"Dammit," he yelped and glanced around frantically. A holobarrier sprang from the ground and he flung himself over it as the projectile landed a few yards away. Thankfully, he managed to escape the main blast but was temporarily blinded when the grenade detonated. He crouched low and clutched his arm in an attempt to ease the searing pain that bit into his flesh.

Kaiden grimaced. "Ow, what the hell?"

"*Flare grenade. It creates a bright light and a heat wave. Barriers don't stop those.*"

"Right...right, damn..." He growled his displeasure and sat. "Still, some forewarning would have been nice. He used basic practice rounds before." He scrambled to his feet and hopped in place for a moment as his body spasmed slightly from the shock.

Chief's eye narrowed. "*Hey, you were the one who wanted*

to see what he had," he reminded him. *"Besides, that was a practice round—technically."*

"All I said was I wanted something a little different. I didn't realize that was on the table."

"This is not going well for you," the EI muttered.

"I've noticed," Kaiden retorted and rubbed his arm. "But wait until you see this—"

As Wolfson pulled the trigger and launched the final grenade, the ace vaulted up and fired while in motion. A blast from his weapon struck the grenade squarely and the device bounced off the mat at an angle, directly at the giant. Before he could rejoice over his certain victory, his adversary simply caught the grenade and lobbed it behind him a split second before it exploded.

"Oh, shit," Kaiden muttered.

"I'll give you the points for skill and say that was impressive," Chief conceded. *"But what he did was off the charts."*

"Yeah, and my ass is grass now." He grasped a grenade on his belt. "I should simply go for it. There's nothing worse than waiting around for a beating."

"Godspeed, you crazy bastard," Chief acknowledged and chuckled.

He sprinted at the giant who threw his launcher over his shoulder and readied to fight. But instead of a direct blow, the younger man slid between the head officer's legs and threw the grenade back. It opened and ensnared the target in a net that immediately constricted around the massive figure.

Wolfson was enveloped from his chest down and he cursed and immediately struggled against the snare. The mesh shifted slightly but held taut, but he was able to keep himself on his feet while his legs strained against his bonds.

Kaiden decided not to waste the opportunity. He fired his remaining shots and the volley finally forced his opponent back slightly. Unfortunately, he had to leap upward to actually strike the man's face, but he used his momentum well to pound into Wolfson with everything he had. The giant continued his struggle to free himself but was finally forced to the mat. The ace managed a less than perfect chokehold, but it did enable him to hammer repeated blows to his adversary's head.

Wolfson's face was bloody and bruised and his eyes were closed. There was no way to tell whether he was conscious or not, but it would be stupid to assume anything considering who it was.

"So, do you give up, big guy?" Kaiden asked. He panted as he pulled against his trainer's neck and sweat dripped from him. It had been a while since he'd had a good fight and he was exhausted, but he had to admit that nothing got his blood pumping like a spar with the less than gentle giant.

"Is that the best you can do?" his opponent asked and hawked blood onto Kaiden's face.

"Are you kidding me? What can you do now? How are you even talking?" he demanded.

"That was a neat little trick that worked better than the first time, at least," Wolfson huffed at his trainee. "But I told you before. You should have kept up with your training." In one swift motion, he headbutted the would-be victor who sprawled off him. He snuck a blade from under his bracer and used it to slice through the net so he could stand. His grin broad, he rolled his shoulders and spat another small blob of blood.

The ace retreated warily. He dragged deep breaths in and balled his fists but kept his expression neutral. "Although," the head officer added, "I suppose I should say congratulations. You landed some solid hits."

"Well, that's a small silver lining." He chuckled, his gaze focused on his trainer. "But I'll still be the winner here."

"You have nothing if not your dreams, boyo," the giant mocked before he suddenly hurtled forward and closed the distance incredibly fast despite his injuries.

Kaiden was too worn out to dodge quickly enough. Instead, he allowed his opponent to rush in close before he stepped to the side and used the man's momentum against him. Unfortunately, as Wolfson flipped, he caught the ace's arm in a vice-like grip and hauled him along for the ride. Their feet had no sooner found the mat than the giant spun and hurled his unwilling passenger like a ragdoll. The hard impact forced the air from Kaiden's lungs, and he grunted with real pain. Despite the mat, he felt like he'd collided with a freight train.

He rolled and recovered quickly, but when he opened his eyes, Wolfson's fist rocketed toward him like a meteorite on steroids. Instinctively, he ducked and raised his arms to lessen the blow, but the force behind the punch was much harder than any strike the man had dealt before. Pain rippled through him as the beefy hand connected with his meager defense and careened him back to roll off the mat and into a table, which he immediately propelled along with him into the far wall.

Wolfson was no longer holding back. It was about time, too.

Kaiden planted a hand on the floor and tried to push himself up. He finally managed to sit and leaned against the wall to drag in ragged breaths. The giant marched toward him, and the ace shook his head and used the wall to steady himself as he stood. Damned if he would have his ass beaten while seated. He slid and lost his balance, but as he prepared to stand once again, his hand connected with something. A quick glance at what it was brought a smile to his face.

He finally straightened, one hand resting on the wall for support, and opened one eye. Wolfson towered over him, his gaze like stone, and blood trickled down his face. "So, do you give?" the man asked, and his low, threatening tone made it difficult to tell if he was mocking him or dead serious.

The ace placed one hand behind his back and motioned with the other for his opponent to attack. "Come at me, you bastard," he challenged.

"You still have the spirit, I'll give you that." The large man drew his arm back. "Well, I guess I'll have to knock it out of you."

As he moved to deliver what he obviously believed was the final blow, the trainee sidestepped him and tossed up a Tesla grenade that had been knocked off the table. He was behind his adversary when it went off but didn't escape entirely. Wolfson took the brunt of the blast, however, and before he could recover, Kaiden spun and forced himself to move despite the fatigue and pain. He delivered a lethal kick into the giant's back with all the power he could muster, and the man careened headfirst into the wall.

The head officer collapsed and Kaiden dropped seconds after. When the giant remained motionless, he took the chance to catch his breath. "So…do you give now?" he asked and grinned when Wolfson groaned.

The man placed a hand on the ground and tried to flip himself over. "I heard you hit the mat, so we're both down now, as I see it."

"Huh. You're gonna be that petty?" the ace jeered. He took a deep breath and pushed to his knees where he paused a moment to muster his remaining strength and stood tall. The head officer finally managed to roll onto his back and squinted up at the triumphant soldier.

"Do you want to call this a win?" he asked and folded his arms, a smirk on his face despite the obvious injuries. "Take a couple of steps," he said and motioned belligerently with his hand.

Kaiden frowned. "Really?"

His horrified tone teased a laugh from his battered opponent. "All right. Fine, boyo, this one is yours."

The ace broke into a full smile before he collapsed onto the mat. "Finally."

They both simply sat and laughed together for a moment before Wolfson added, "You know this still makes it thirty-four to one in my favor, right?"

"Fine, fuck it. I'll take it."

CHAPTER SEVEN

The ace lay on the medbay cot and relaxed as the effects of Dr. Soni's patented "blue stuff" did its thing. It had been a while since he'd enjoyed the good doctor's little proprietary blend, but it didn't take long for him to remember why he appreciated it so much.

"Are you feeling better, Kaiden?" a soft voice asked. He opened an eye as Dr. Soni approached, her hand raised in a polite wave.

"Very much so, thanks, Doc." He adjusted his head to get comfortable and closed his eye. "It's been a while. Did you miss me?"

"This might come as something of a shock, but as much as I enjoy helping people, my job is to get them back on their feet so they don't have to spend that much time in here," she related and placed a tablet on the stand beside him. "How are you feeling?"

"Good...pretty damn good." He sighed. "How's Wolfson?"

"He's already discharged himself. I'm sure you know

he's not much of a fan of hospitals." She sat on the edge of his bed. "You really did a number on him, though."

"I took him down this time," Kaiden declared proudly. "It's actually the first time I've won one of our little matches."

"So, what does that make the score?"

He shifted slightly again and craned his neck to look at her. "I think he said the score was thirty-four to one, now."

"So you still have a climb, then." she chuckled and shook her head. "But please, try not to come down here each and every time you fight. It's not like you get a free ice cream cone after a certain number of visits."

"That would make a nice addition," he mused.

Dr. Soni motioned to the tablet. "I received a message from Commander Sasha. It appears he's been looking for you."

"He can't have looked very hard," he said and flexed his hand a few times to ease the stiffness. "I really only go to maybe five places on this island."

"One of which is here," she pointed out. "When you're feeling better, head over to his office asap."

"I gotcha." Kaiden nodded. "Hey, Doc, before you go, have you given this stuff a name yet?"

"The serum?" she asked. "I wasn't going to bother until I released it for general use, but I've kicked around a few ideas. I'm mostly partial to K brew."

"K brew? What does that stand for?"

"What do you think?" she retorted as she stood and walked away. "Kaiden's brew."

"Can I help you?" a man in the Nexus offices lobby asked. Neither his tone nor his expression indicated any particular desire to be helpful.

"I'm Adva Kaiden Jericho. I've been told to report to Commander Sasha's office."

The official looked at his tablet and scanned through it for a moment before he nodded and gestured for him to proceed. "Take the elevator to the sixth floor. Your EI can guide you to his office, but head directly there and only there."

"Right." Kaiden walked briskly past him and over to the elevators. He called one down and entered, pressed the key for the sixth floor, and waited for the ascent.

"What do you think he wants?" Chief asked.

"I don't know. It's been a while since we talked face to face," he responded thoughtfully. "Maybe he only wants to catch-up."

"After all this time, he really strikes you as a guy who likes to shoot the breeze?"

"Hey, other than that, I have no idea." The elevator reached the sixth floor, and Kaiden took his lenses out and put them on as the doors opened. Chief generated a directional line to follow to the commander's office.

"Do you think you're in trouble?" the EI asked after a moment.

"What is this? A daycare?" The ace scoffed. "I think I would have to report to the chancellor or something if it was extreme, but let's not jump to conclusions." He rounded the corner, approached the commander's office, and knocked on the door. No one responded until a blue, glowing owl appeared above him.

"Uh...hello," he greeted the EI, whose eyes circled in its head.

"Hello there, Adva Jericho. I am Commander Sasha's personal EI assistant Isaac. It's a pleasure to meet you. I've seen you before, of course, but this is our first formal introduction."

"Cool...um, nice to meet you, Isaac," Kaiden acknowledged as Chief popped out to look at the owl.

"You weren't so polite during our first meeting, Kaiden," he accused and spun around the commander's EI.

"To be fair, neither were you," he retorted cheekily before he returned his attention to Isaac. "I heard Sasha is looking for me?"

"Indeed. Allow me to get the door." No sooner had the EI disappeared when the door to the commander's office opened. It was surprisingly dark in the room despite it being only the afternoon. A couple of lamps were on and the windows were covered.

Kaiden walked in and the door closed behind him. "Sasha, are you here?"

"Over here, Kaiden," the commander's voice responded. The ace approached a small, round table in the corner, where Sasha sat in a chair with his back to him and looked intently at something on a holoscreen. "I'm glad you could make it so promptly."

"Well, I thought it must be important if you called me here directly." He eased into the chair opposite the commander, hooked an arm along the back of it, and cocked his head questioningly. "So, what do you need?"

His host responded by taking a scroll device from his pocket and tossing it wordlessly at him. He snatched it out of the air and scanned it quickly. "This looks like... A contract?" He looked at the commander in surprise. "You got me a gig?"

"On occasion, I still get a few across my desk—not for me to perform, of course, but for advice or to pass along." Sasha completed his work and deactivated the holoscreen. "This seemed to be up your alley."

Kaiden returned his attention to the scroll. "A reconnaissance mission, potential retrieval if an item of interest is identified, and shouldn't take more than a night." He looked up and nodded. "The pay is good too, but with the test coming up..." He shrugged and let the gesture finish his sentence for him.

"I understand." Sasha waved dismissively. "It's merely something I thought I should bring to your attention,"

He held his hands up, mainly because he felt he needed to be honest and he didn't want the other man to make incorrect assumptions. "No, no, I appreciate it but...well, previous engagements and the fact that... Okay, to be honest, I thought this might be some sort of test."

Sasha linked his hands together. "If it was, you tipped your hand a little early."

"I didn't wanna come across like a dick," the ace admitted. "But you've never really shown any interest in my extracurriculars before now."

"Maybe because I originally thought it was a way for you to acquire finances before you graduated. But once I realized the types of missions you were undertaking, and the risks and rewards those missions entailed, I realized you were doing more than simply getting yourself fiscally buoyant."

A couple of beads of sweat appeared on his brow. "Uh,

yeah, you might be on the right track. But I did look into the Academy rules and they said nothing about trying to buy out my own contract."

The commander nodded, picked up a glass of water, and sipped from it slowly. "So, that is what you are looking to do."

He blinked rapidly in confusion. "Yeah…wasn't that where you were leading?"

"Certainly. But that was purely guesswork. I can only assume so much without your confirmation." He took another sip as the words sank in. Kaiden groaned and knocked the palm of his hand against his head in frustration.

Chief chortled in the back of his mind. *You fell for the oldest trick in the book, dumbass.*

"Yeah, yeah, quiet down," Kaiden grumbled. "So, are you trying to talk me out of it? I don't see why. Either way, the Academy gets its money. It's not like I'd scam you, or is it an honor thing?"

"No, nothing like that. I have no intention of stopping you, Kaiden," Sasha assured him. "I called you in here to satiate my curiosity."

The ace finally relaxed a little and kicked his feet up on the table. "I can try, I guess, but about what exactly?"

"I assume that you plan to buy out your contract once you graduate," the commander ventured.

"I thought that if I did so beforehand, that would be plain dumb," he admitted. "If I did that, what would keep me here?"

"You mean besides the fact that would mean you essentially paid for your own education like you would at every other college?" Sasha pointed out.

A fairly long silence was followed by a sigh that spoke to Kaiden's feeling of idiocy. "I guess Mia's whole speech on the first day made me think that the contracts were a big deal. If you couldn't sell me off, I didn't have much value."

"This Academy does make its own profit, yes, but we don't look at you all as simple cattle," Sasha grunted with evident disapproval. "Perhaps we should have a conversation at the next faculty meeting about making that clearer."

"Or it might simply be my personal paranoia," he admitted. "Plus, I never brought it up because I wasn't even sure it would work. I have a three-million-credit debt, but the whole idea of the contract is that you sell them to a company for well over what they are worth, right? They might not even accept me buying myself out. I couldn't find any records of it happening before."

"I can tell you that it has happened before—under special circumstances," Sasha stated quietly. "That's why I want you to be clear on what you plan to do. I could be a potential asset in your plan."

"Really, you would do that for me?"

"Again, that depends on you." The commander placed his glass on the table and folded his hands again. "Have you thought that far?"

Kaiden took a deep breath. "Honestly, if you had asked a month ago, I would have said not really, but I have knocked an idea around."

"Then let's hear it."

He nodded and coughed into his hand to hide his

nervousness before he spoke. "A merc company. I've thought of starting a mercenary group." He tensed when he saw the other man's brow furrow. "I know they don't usually have the greatest reputations—well, morally, at any rate. Guys like the Omega Horde and Red Suns certainly have great reputations for destruction and the like."

"Among other unsavory things, yes." Sasha nodded. "Most merc groups are run more like terrorist organizations or interstellar gangs than what their original purpose was intended to be."

"Yeah, but I plan to bring it back to basics," the ace explained. "Look, I don't know what you think about gangs, but you took a chance on me and I can tell you that mine was at least somewhat respectable. We did a lot of good."

The commander moved a hand across his chest as if to straighten or brush lint off his jacket. "I'm not one who thinks every gang or collective is nefarious."

"I know I have two years left, but even with that, I don't think I'll exactly be cut out for typical military leadership."

"What makes you think you would get a leadership role?"

"Come on, I'm an ace. That's the job description," Kaiden countered. "And yes, before you say it, I know that I can still change classes. But I have been adjusting to the whole leader thing in my own way. I don't hate the idea anymore, at least."

"So, by creating your own merc group, you would be able to lead 'in your own way,' then?"

"Exactly." He nodded. "I've made some great connections—no, friends—in this Academy. Perhaps, if I build up a good reputation and get the credits rolling in, I could get them to come on board in time."

"That's rather optimistic," Sasha noted dryly before he showed a sliver of a smile. "But I like the thought you've put into it."

"So you don't think it's daft?" Kaiden asked hopefully.

"You could stand to think it over in more detail. And you'll need to make further progress than simply buying your contract out."

"Like what?"

"Look into getting a ship. You'll get more bounties and jobs in space, along with better rewards. Plus, the merc business is somewhat oversaturated here on Earth, which is not a good prospect to the board."

The ace considered this carefully. "I follow...maybe I can get Julio to see what he can find. In fact, there might be — I'll leave it be until I find out for sure."

Sasha was intrigued by what Kaiden was thinking, but he let it lie. "So, where do you go from here?" The young man was silent. "Kaiden?"

"Huh? Oh, sorry, Sasha. I was thinking. Unless you have any further questions, I'll think about it and come back to you later. I wanted to get a quick trip in the Animus before I head to bed."

"Understood. This was a good talk." The older man stood and offered his hand.

"It was enlightening," Kaiden said and shook firmly. "And thanks, Sasha—again."

"Keep it up and I'll be happy to help any way I can," he promised and clasped his hands behind his back. "That is what I'm here for, after all."

The ace smiled as he made his way out and turned to wave as the doors shut. No sooner was he out of view than Sasha sighed and collapsed into the chair. He pounded a fist into the armrest.

Without a doubt, he should have used this opportunity to tell him what was in store, but he couldn't bring himself to do it. Kaiden deserved his help—for all that he had done and was about to do.

Without having a clue about what it all involved.

CHAPTER EIGHT

G in, as Egon, strolled through the halls of the Animus Center. More memories of his time at the Academy drifted through his mind to highlight the changes in a way that wasn't altogether comfortable. They had really made quite a few upgrades in the decade-plus since he had been away, hadn't they?

The center housed almost seven hundred pods now, along with improved tech and décor—which even his emotionally jaundiced eye had to admit really improved the atmosphere.

As he passed one of the halls, he received an alert and a picture of Kaiden popped up in the HUD of his oculars. He stopped in his tracks and turned his head slowly to look into the hall. No one was there—at least outside the pods, so he crept forward and to the left. His HUD directed him all the way down near the end to a pod that was in use.

There he was, right in front of him—the target of his mission and one of those who got away.

For a while, anyway.

JOSHUA ANDERLE & MICHAEL ANDERLE

The killer circled the pod and examined the various cables and devices attached to it before he stopped in front of it again. He could simply end this there. His hand moved instinctually to the blade on his waist and grasped at nothing but the belt. Right, he hadn't brought it with him this time.

He walked back to the side of the pod and traced two fingers along one of the wires. Was there a way to short it out? Maybe he could use the blackout mod, but that would mean he would race against the system failsafe. It would probably desync the student before it caused any real damage.

Gin took a deep breath and stepped away. No, he decided. Not here and not now. This was about more than Kaiden, although he would have his part to play—the sacrificial pawn. He looked up at a monitor above the pod that showed the ace in the middle of a firefight. He easily dispatched a group of mercs with some kind of pack on his back. In all honesty, he had to give him some credit. He was quite capable when not pursued by an infamous revenant.

But he usually had that effect on people. Somehow, they always delivered less than their best when they confronted him.

Footsteps caught his attention and he walked swiftly to the end of the row of pods as a trio of students entered to prepare for a mission. The killer's eyes narrowed when he saw the symbol of an exotech on the jacket arm of one of the students.

Before the memory behind that could fully crystallize, a soft click behind him announced a pod disengaging. He glanced casually back to see Kaiden's pod open and he flinched. Rather than move away, he remained where he was. His target wouldn't be able to tell who he was, and maybe he should have a final conversation with the boy.

Last rites of some kind. It had a pleasant ring to it.

The killer approached as Kaiden stepped out of the pod and stretched. "A good performance, Kaiden."

The ace rolled his neck and gave Gin a puzzled look. "Thanks, but have we met?"

"In a way." He nodded and offered his hand. "I'm Doctor Egon. I work in the tech department under professor Laurie. We met during some of your visits with the professor, but for only a few moments."

"Oh! Well, I'm sorry I didn't notice. Honestly, I'm not the greatest with faces," he apologized and shook the proffered hand. "Are you making the rounds? Or is there something wrong with the pods?"

"No, nothing like that," Gin stated and shook his head. *Not yet, anyway.* "I used to be in charge of setting the pods up here, but it hasn't been my responsibility for a few years now. I suppose I felt a little..." He looked through the gaps between the pods and his gaze settled on the exotech student, who stepped into one a few rows down. "Nostalgic would possibly be the right word. I wanted to take a look around and see the changes to my old stamping grounds. I'm sure you can relate."

Kaiden rubbed the back of his neck. "I guess, in a way. To be totally honest, I haven't thought about taking a trip back to my old stamping grounds in a while."

"No good memories, then?" the killer asked.

"Actually, I have a lot of good memories, but... Sometimes, it only takes one bad memory to mess things up."

Gin froze and balled his fist behind his back. "Yes, I can say I do know."

The ace noticed that the other man had tensed. "Ah, I'm sorry, Doc. I didn't mean to make you feel bad. I'm rambling. Coming out of the pod always makes me woozy for a while."

"It's all right, Kaiden. It's not your fault—although sometimes, that doesn't mean you don't have to deal with the fallout," he said cryptically.

"Do what now?" Kaiden asked and folded his arms. "Is rambling a thing with most techs?"

"I suppose it's a part of the trade, considering how much we deal with potentials and hypothesis." He snickered and took a few steps past the student, walked up to the monitor, and tapped it a few times. "Are you preparing for the upcoming final?"

"Yeah, practicing doing solo stuff. It's been a while since I've had a solo test, but I've done other things solo, though. Still, they like to throw weird things at us from time to time." The ace cocked his head thoughtfully. "Although I guess, since you work in tech, you would be one of those people who craft those weird things, wouldn't ya?"

Gin shrugged. "We like to keep you on your toes. Plus, we have a lot of time to imagine those scenarios." He turned his attention back to the student. "Are you looking forward to running solo again?"

"Sure, but it's not like I've been dying for one or anything."

"No, I suppose not, but you seem smart enough to

know that you should always rely on your own skills rather than depend on the help of others."

The ace regarded the technician in confusion. "Uh... you do realize that this is an academy filled with the best of the best, right? Of course, we can all have a bad day, but I've run through any number of missions and tests with others and they've always gone well." He stopped himself for a moment and thought it over. "For the most part, anyway. Plus, this whole year was spent getting us to work together more."

"And yet your final test is a solo mission," the killer pointed out. "You won't be able to rely on others this time around. I'm simply recommending that you should learn that as a rule in life, not only in these games."

"You're kind of nihilistic for a doctor, aren't ya?" Kaiden muttered and folded his arms. "You work with people all the time, right? Even lead them? I'm an ace. People rely on me to lead at times as well."

Gin sighed and shook his head. "I suppose my words of wisdom are lost on the youth of today."

"I'm merely saying that you have to have at least some people you trust, right? Maybe one or two?"

He turned away and stared over his shoulder. "At one time, I had a few, yes. I still stand by what I say, however."

The ace hesitated. Part of him wanted to continue butting heads with this techie, but he could tell there was some damage there and sighed. "Whatever happened, I guess I'll say I'm sorry about it. But come on, man, if you didn't have hope for the future or actually believed your all for one mentality, you wouldn't be here, would you?"

The killer laughed. "Perhaps, but I suppose I'll simply

say that I have my personal reasons for being here, and I can accomplish them myself." He began to walk away but stopped at the end of the row and called back to Kaiden as he placed a hand on one of the pods. "Keep it up, Kaiden, and have a little fun while you're at it. You never know how much time you have left." With that, he turned and left the hall.

"Well, that started out nice enough, but now, I feel chilly," Chief grumbled.

"Can you even feel temperature?" Kaiden asked and unconsciously rubbed one of his arms.

"I can make a good guess. Plus, its metaphor anyway, asshat," Chief retorted. *"It's not really like you to have an existential discussion with randos. Are you feelin' all right, partner?"*

"I guess I was caught up in the conversation." He shrugged as if he could shake off the odd feeling of disquiet. "Plus, I felt like I knew him. The face wasn't familiar, but the…vibe, for lack of a better word, was familiar, if rather off-putting."

"Looking back through the logs, we've seen Egon a few times at the R&D center and he's usually present at the big get-togethers. He was at the auditorium yesterday and eyeballed you intently a few times too."

"In a bad way?" the ace asked. "Maybe it's a career thing? Do you think he might have bad blood with Laurie? And me by proxy considering I'm his little project?"

"Technically, I'm his little project," Chief corrected. *"You're merely the box I'm in."*

"Are you gonna call him daddy too?" Kaiden jibed. "If so, I'm out." A message popped up on his screen. "It looks like Chiyo is trying to get in touch."

"It's getting late. Maybe we should take a rain check."

Kaiden waved a hand airily. "Eh, it shouldn't take too long. Besides, it's been a while since the two of us had a simple conversation."

"I guess we can see what she wants. Besides, I personally enjoy it when she calls you on your bullshit." The EI chortled.

"I haven't done anything," he countered and slid his hands into his jacket pockets. "I swear, you're looking for me to get in trouble nowadays."

Chief spun in the HUD and turned a pleased pink. *"Maybe a little, but to your credit, it's happened less and less. I'm almost beginning to think you've become respectable."*

Kaiden laughed. "We wouldn't want that now, would we?"

CHAPTER NINE

K aiden stood beside the fountain in the academy
plaza and looked around for Chiyo. "How did I
beat her here when she was the one who called me?"

"You could always look for her on the network map," Chief
reminded him. *"Hell, let me do it. Honestly, it will take literally
a second."*

"Nah, I'll quit my welching." He removed his jacket and
slung it over his shoulder. "She would send a message if
she—"

"Hello, Kaiden," Chiyo said and he almost stumbled into
the fountain in surprise.

"Jesus, did you put some synapse points into assassina-
tion or something?" he demanded.

"That's not a real skill," she responded and sat on the
rim of the fountain. "Not technically, although I suppose
you could put points into stealth, melee weapons, or get
the proper mods to—"

"You're taking this too far when you just said it's not a
thing." He chuckled. "What did you want to talk about?"

"I wanted to pass this along to you," she said and held a drive up for him.

Kaiden took it and frowned at it in confusion. "What's this for? Some assignments I missed?"

"I would assume I'd need more storage for that." She deadpanned but still teased a laugh from him. "It's a set of maps I downloaded for you to help prepare for your tests."

Kaiden glanced at the drive again. "Wow, I'm touched." He placed the device into his back pants pocket. "Thanks, Chi. I'm sorry to say I haven't got anything like that for you."

"You've helped me considerably over the last couple of years," she stated, her gaze on the rising moon in the evening sky. "This was where we met on your first day here."

"Yeah, it is." He glanced over his shoulder at the fountain. "You know, thinking back, those guys who picked on you that night…I haven't seen them bothering you since the end of last year."

"One of them washed out during the last test and failed teamwork exercises one too many times," she explained.

He scoffed. "That's not hard to believe."

"The others seem to have moved beyond their petty grievances. I suppose I proved to them that I do belong here. While it doesn't make what they thought any better, time and action do help in dealing with troubles."

Kaiden was silent for a moment and scuffed his boot along the ground as he considered his next question carefully. "You know, you never did tell me why you were such a loner during those first few months, or why anyone had problems with you."

"Do you think they are connected?" Chiyo asked quietly.

"I ain't exactly a detective, but considering that you were personally invited to come here and had some of the highest marks of anyone last year, I can only guess that it was either jealousy or there was something shady going on." He caught his next words and turned to her. "Not that I think you did anything malicious, and while rumors can grow into horrible things, they start from somewhere."

She closed her eyes. "You don't need to fret, Kaiden, but tell me—what have you heard?"

Kaiden folded his jacket on the side of the fountain and sat beside her. "I try not to listen to gossip, but from the tidbits you've mentioned, you grew up hacking, may come from wealth, and came here looking for a 'path' or something cryptic like that."

The infiltrator smiled. "Yes, I remember our first conversation. You were more...bitter back then."

"I had more of a chip on my shoulder," he admitted sheepishly. "In my defense, I had Chief shoved into my head just before we met. I was a little grumpy."

"Well, it was great to see you relax over time and mature along the way." She smiled. "How do you think your journey has gone? Have you found your path?"

"I'm making one," he stated and placed the palms of his hands on the edge of the fountain so he could lean back and gaze into the sky. "I'm not really sure I have the destination down properly, but I'm making a path to something." He blinked and turned his attention to her once more. "I thought we were talking about you."

Chiyo nodded. "We were—not my favorite subject. I

suppose it's a habit to try to divert attention." She sighed and avoided his gaze. "It is basically an unspoken rule that after your second year at an ark academy, it's the metaphorical point of no return. From here on, you're locked into the path you've chosen."

"I would have thought that happened way back when they slapped you with a multi-million-credit contract." Kaiden grimaced.

"There are scholarships and workarounds that allow you to leave the Academy and reduce the amount you have to pay. It's still not a great situation but more realistic than doing it later," she explained. "But it's semantics. In reality, there have been people who left in their last year. It's simply one of those things that had enough coincidences to be believed as fact after a while."

He eyed the infiltrator, his lips pursed. "Are you thinking of leaving, Chi?"

She met his gaze at last. "It occurred to me, but that was long ago—before I met everyone, I thought that the skills I had were enough to start a life in the field of my choice. I didn't see the point in developing those skills further only to be bound to some company for years."

"I can't say I don't see that logic. It's something I've thought about a lot myself," he admitted. "But you moved past that eventually?"

"As I said, it was before I met everyone. Specifically, those thoughts left my mind after our test together."

"The Co-op Test?" he asked. "Why that one specifically?"

"It was the first time in a quite a while that I was forced to trust someone, and they came through," Chiyo stated.

Kaiden was taken aback before she raised a hand and knocked a knuckle against his forehead. "In your own catastrophic way."

"You're never gonna let me have a nice moment, are you?" he grumbled sarcastically as he rubbed his head, although he did manage a smile.

"You've gotten better, and to be honest, I've grown to enjoy it," she admitted. "But only sometimes. Don't let yourself think you can go back to simply blowing everything up."

"It's still always my plan C," he countered.

"At least it's not plan A anymore." She giggled, crossed her legs, and leaned back. "I guess I'm steering the conversation away from me again, aren't I?"

"Yeah, but to be fair, talking about me is a good way to do that," Kaiden teased with a smirk. "I enjoy it, at least, but I would like to know more about you. All my knowledge is basically current. I can't say I know how you came to be... well, you."

"Lots of studying and little social life, for the most part," Chiyo stated. "At least, a social life that wasn't constantly watched and scrutinized."

"Were your parents overprotective?"

"My father, specifically. My mother was...not around, for the most part,"

Kaiden felt a sense of guilt creeping in. "Hey, while I would certainly like to hear more, I don't want you to bring up something that's...not pleasant. I already did that earlier with one of the techs."

"No, it's all right," she assured him. "Besides, it would be a quite short conversation if I avoided anything that was slightly unpleasant." She activated a holoscreen, opened a file with pictures, and displayed a large building that glowed with bright lights. It was built in Janeo style with spiraled pillars, angled windows, and arched corners, and looked essentially like a modern version of imperial Japanese architecture. "This is the Fantaji corporation primary building, one of the leading companies in modern technology—specifically, computing, modifications, and robotics. It is the center of the Mirai Zaibatsu and is owned and run by Gendo Orikasa, my father."

"You're the heir to the Mirai Zaibatsu?" He was genuinely astonished. "That...uh, only raises more questions. Like why you are here instead of preparing to be a multi-trillionaire, and why you learned to hack instead of going to a premier business school."

"I'm not the heir and never was," she stated. "I was born out of wedlock and my father never acknowledged me as his daughter."

"What?" Kaiden asked, aghast. "How is that even possible? You couldn't have been kept hidden all those years. Did he keep you in a dungeon or something?"

"No, I was a ward, legally. You can look up articles from years ago about how he adopted me out of the kindness of his heart after visiting one of the orphanages he supports in his various charities," she explained. "I mentioned that my mother wasn't around a lot. That was because she passed away early on in my life, and my father took me in once that happened. I don't want to paint him as an evil or apathetic man. He was there when he needed to be, and I understand that I was and am fortunate compared to many others. But I never felt that I was truly connected to him. It was one of the reasons—maybe the primary reason—that I started learning to hack."

"It was for your father?" he asked.

"Technically, it was for the company," she confirmed. "It shouldn't surprise you that a company whose primary trade is technology would worry about security, so highly skilled hackers and crackers were sought after. I learned under the tutelage of several mentors and I surpassed them by the time I was in my early teens. During those times— when I could find the problems in the systems of the company's devices and impress my father—it was a euphoric feeling." She was silent as she used the moment to think about her past and sigh over moments lost. "But those feelings lessened after a time. I reached a point where I felt like I was no better than a machine. I went from looking for approval to developing a Rubix complex. I needed to solve the puzzle purely for the satisfaction."

"And that's what brought you here? You saw no future there?"

"Not one that would please me," she said despondently. "I said that I wasn't ever recognized as my father's daughter. The big reason is that in that environment—in Zaibatsus like that—nepotism is the norm. I would have been the one to take over once my father stepped down, but considering the potential scandal that would have resulted given my lineage and my mother's specifically—"

"You're a Hāfu," Kaiden interrupted and earned a curious glance from Chiyo. "I've picked up quite a few terms in my life. The derogatory ones were unfortunately quite common in gang life."

"I don't see it as derogatory," she retorted.

"My bad," he apologized. "But my guess is that enough people do that it posed a problem."

Chiyo fell silent before she released a quick, amused snort and startled him. "You say you're no detective, but you're quite perceptive when you want to be."

"I've heard stories like yours before," he responded and rapped his knuckles on the fountain edge. "It's a damn shame to be treated like that. Tradition is horseshit."

"Tradition has its place," she said and shook her head firmly. "But yes, that would be the main reason I could not step up to the head position. My father gave no indication that it was a personal belief, but the board and shareholders...well, enough of them had the problem that it made it an impossibility—for now."

"And you had no desire to change it?" the ace asked.

"I'm sure I could have found a place in the company, as a hacker or otherwise, but I decided to pursue my own opportunities. Fortunately, around that time, I received the invitation to come here and I took it."

Kaiden couldn't find the words to adequately respond. Her story was heavier than he'd expected. But then again, it explained why she hadn't spoken about it until now, at least. "Thank you for sharing,"

"I'm sorry if it was a—" she began but he stopped her quickly with a finger to her lips.

"Nah, don't mention it. I asked, even though it's a little complex for me. I'm glad you felt you could share with me."

She looked at him and nodded before she returned her attention to the sky. "Thank you for listening."

"It's what I do, I know when to shut up—from time to time." They shared a companionable silence for a while until another question stirred in the back of his mind. "So, did you find your path?"

"I thought I had, but it seems to change from time to time." She sighed.

"It's more tricky than you'd thought it would be, huh?" he joked.

"I suppose I said that with a little arrogance the first time."

"You? Nah." Kaiden waved off. "Maybe a bit overconfident, but I couldn't speak to that at all, being so modest."

She chuckled. "Of course, your best-known quality."

He smiled. "But do you have any regrets that the path changed?"

She looked at him and grinned. "I'm still walking, aren't I?"

CHAPTER TEN

The night sky was illuminated by the torches and festive lights of the Academy Plaza. Almost all the advanced class was there on the night of the annual finals feast. It also looked like there were more dishes than last year. These included more Tsuna dishes and what the students were told was a sampling of Sauren and Mirus 'inspired' dishes for the first time ever.

A few brave souls did try the Sauren dishes, which seemed like slabs of meat with odd toppings and sauces. But the Mirus ones were left untouched—how did an alien race without mouths actually eat? Or were their mouths merely not on their faces? Too many questions like these tended to make people a little unadventurous.

Kaiden took his plates of meats and sides to the trio of tables where his group had gathered. He sat between Chiyo and Genos. This year, he'd chosen to be responsible and hadn't asked for any hard alcohol. He put the bottle of beer to his lips and guzzled half of it in almost one swallow.

"Friends, I believe we should place some bets this year,"

Genos suggested and grinned at those around the table. "An attempt to be sporting. Who here will have the best score?"

"Well, it depends," Jaxon said cautiously. "Considering the fact that each test is suited to the individual talents of each class and the student's individual skills, there may be different opportunities for point accumulation that other classes won't—"

"I'll bet on me," Kaiden said with a cocky smirk.

"Is that right?" Flynn chuckled, took out his EI device, and placed it beside his plate. "I guess that would be the smart place to put your creds, but don't think I've simply been resting on my laurels all year, ain't that right, Jeeves?"

"Yes indeed, Mr. Flynn," the well-dressed kangaroo EI responded. The furry avatar boasted a new bowtie.

"Is that something festive for the evening, Flynn?" the ace asked and gestured with his fork.

"He insisted on dressing up." The marksman shrugged.

"Dressing up? He's a Kangaroo in a tux," Raul protested.

"Maybe I should download new outfits for Chief. I need to see what they have for a fancy lightbulb," Kaiden mused

"I look good enough as I am, thank you very much," Chief chirped and appeared in the air.

"Can you even be considered good-looking if you're a floating eye?" Kaiden wondered aloud, his grin taunting.

"To be fair, I compared myself to you, so that's an easy bar to fly over," Chief jibed and earned a glare.

"Good evening, Chief," Chiyo greeted the EI, along with a few of the others.

"Evening ladies and gents. Are we feeling good?" he asked. Everyone nodded and some raised their glasses or bottles.

"Is everyone ready? How was the training over the last week?" Jaxon asked.

"I can't complain here and I'm always good to roll," Mack boasted. "By myself or with a team, nothing can stop me."

"I've used some specialized maps and I've progressed more in the last couple of weeks than in the last several months," Chiyo related.

"It's good to have friends in high places, huh?" Kaiden teased. "Between working with Wolfson and running missions almost day in and day out, I'll probably tear through whatever they have in store for me."

"Durand's here," Otto notified the group. They turned to where the chancellor stood at the end of the plaza. Monitor screens activated above them and in the oculars of the students who wore them. Everyone settled quietly as he raised a hand and beckoned for silence.

"Good evening, advas." His greeting drew a few verbal responses from the amassed students. "I hope everyone is enjoying their pre-finals meal and wanted to wish you a brief good luck and…"

Wolfson, Laurie, and Sasha sat in the professor's office and watched the screen as Durand continued his speech. "The chancellor really loves his speeches, doesn't he?" Laurie mused.

"He adheres to rather antiquated thinking when it comes to leadership," Wolfson stated and shrugged his muscled shoulders. "Personally, I prefer to get in and get the job done, myself."

"It's good for morale and works to bolster the face of the Academy," Sasha pointed out.

"Heh, yeah, because that's been a major concern through all this," the giant muttered. "Do you two really have to go through with this?" he asked and changed the subject.

"Technically, it's only me," Laurie huffed and glanced quickly at his monitor screen. "Under the directions of the board, of course, but I know that the dear commander would like nothing more than to trash the whole thing,"

"Then why don't you?" Wolfson demanded. "Do you really think they will let go of it? That you can work your technomancy and hide the fact that it didn't happen?"

"They'll be watching and recording it. The whole reason we agreed to do it was so that this would be the final time we would have to work on this project," Sasha reminded the head officer.

"Yeah, the thirty pieces of silver and all that," Wolfson remarked dourly.

"We gain nothing personal from this, Baioh," the commander countered. "You were even on board when we first explained the project to you years ago."

"Aye, I *was*." He snorted with real disgust. "That was before we started to use our own students as test subjects. It would be one thing if they volunteered, but we simply shoved them into those skin suits without their consent."

"We couldn't risk anyone knowing. As it is, we're already dealing with legal issues and potential espionage when it comes to the Animus," Laurie pointed out. "If something like this got out and the potential capabilities were discovered, what's to stop them from being used for nefarious purposes? Especially when we aren't exactly sure of them ourselves?"

Wolfson glared at the professor before he sighed belligerently and stood. "This'll be the last one? You promise?"

"I swear." Sasha nodded.

"We swear," Laurie added.

The giant nodded without looking back. "Raza is coming through tomorrow, and I have to get the documents ready, so I'll leave with this," the man warned as he walked away. "He'd better get through this all right. I've finally grown fond of him, after all,"

Once the head officer had left, Sasha looked at Laurie. "Are you sure everything is prepared?"

"Of course," his companion assured him. "I even sent one of my personal technicians to make final preparations to be sure." An alert flashed on his monitor and the professor struck a key. "Good timing. Come in."

A man with a five o'clock shadow and short brown hair walked in. "Hello, Raynor. Is everything in order?"

"Yeah. I checked the mainframe, and everything is green," the technician confirmed. "Do you need anything else, sir?"

"No, you are relieved for the evening, but be sure to be here bright and early tomorrow to oversee the mainframe during the tests," Laurie ordered.

"I wouldn't miss it, sir. Have a good one." He nodded and turned to leave, and the doors closed slowly behind him.

JOSHUA ANDERLE & MICHAEL ANDERLE

"I can never read that guy," the professor muttered. He flashed his companion a worried look. "This will be done in twenty-four hours. We're almost out."

"Perhaps in the short term," Sasha whispered. He removed his oculars and looked the man in his eyes. "But eventually, we'll have to tell him."

He nodded and sighed. "Just when I thought he was growing fond of me."

The students in the plaza stood and saluted the chancellor as he departed, and a few ran up to speak to him.

With the night winding down, Julius, Mack, and Otto said their goodbyes and were the first to head back to their respective dorms. The others began to follow suit and wished each other luck with good-natured warnings not to say up too late. Kaiden finished his meal and pushed his plate aside. "That was good."

"Are you sure you didn't consume too many intoxicants, friend Kaiden?" Genos asked with a concerned frown.

"Nah, I'll be good. I have an iron constitution." The ace sipped from his mostly untouched glass of water and glanced at Chiyo, who wore a contemplative look on her face. "Are you all right?"

"You do seem troubled, friend Chiyo. Is there anything we can help with?" Genos asked.

"It's nothing—or at least not anything big." The infiltrator waved her hand dismissively.

"Still, you seemed deep in thought," Kaiden pointed out.

She shifted slightly with what might have been discomfort. "It's about our last test."

"That was months ago," the ace reminded her.

"Some people like to keep things in mind instead of chuck them out as soon as they grow bored with them," Chief huffed.

"I have more things to worry about if you hadn't noticed," he retorted.

"It's only that I noticed a few oddities. I've looked into them on my own time since the end of the test, but I'm not sure if I'm honestly onto something or...well, I might simply be paranoid."

"That doesn't really sound like you," Kaiden noted. "What are you thinking?"

"It's... I don't know...the simulations are realistic, and that's the point. But some of the interactions—like with that merc accountant or whoever that was at the end. He seemed a little off, I guess."

"Yeah, I had a weird interaction with the pirate captain," the ace recalled. "I already talked to Laurie about it, actually. He said that some of the missions were used as testing grounds for a potential update, specifically the ones based on real missions from the archives, rather than recreations."

"He revealed that to you?" Genos asked with some surprise.

"Laurie is chatty." He deadpanned.

Chiyo tapped her fork on her empty plate. "Okay. I guess that makes sense. It's not like real missions or environments like that would be filled with robotic-acting mercs, at least not the ones without androids."

"It sounds like a leap forward in Animus design," Genos

said as he tapped his infuser absently. "Although it seems realistic as it is now. Tsuna students even have infusers in their armor following the latest upgrades."

"It was merely something that piqued my curiosity," she admitted. "I suppose I was caught off-guard, but the update makes sense. It's strange, though, that they didn't announce it beforehand."

"Maybe they were concerned that too many students would dick around to see what was different instead of actually completing their mission," Kaiden suggested. "My guess is they'll make an announcement next year."

"It's getting close to bedtime, Kaiden," Chief interjected.

"Thanks, glorified alarm clock," he responded jokingly.

"Cute, I'll keep that in mind." Chief's tone had a foreboding edge to it.

"What's that now?"

"We should get to sleep and prepare for tomorrow." The infiltrator stacked her plates and stood quickly. "I'm sure I'll see you tomorrow, but just in case, good luck."

The trio wished one another a good night. Raynor looked on from the shadows and smiled as he sauntered away. When he was sure that it would go unnoticed, his face morphed into Egon's dull and unimpressive features.

CHAPTER ELEVEN

K aiden was awoken by what sounded like a massive bomb. He sat hastily and his head smacked on the top of his pod. "Ow, what the hell?"

"Goooood morning!" Chief yelled merrily. *"Good morning, good morning, good morning. It's time to rise and shine."*

"What the hell is wrong with you? You nearly gave me a heart attack," he grumbled and rubbed the decidedly tender place on his head.

"You did call me a 'glorified alarm clock,'" the EI reminded him. *"I thought I'd simply get into character."*

The ace activated the switch to open the pod, pushed out, and stretched. "Man, you didn't hold onto that for long."

"While I like to catch you unawares, I'm sure you'll give me enough opportunities in the future." Chief chuckled. *"Now, hurry up and get dressed. Let's get going, future master."*

His frown turned to a smile. "Yeah, yeah. All right, partner."

The day has come. Gin was focused on the mainframe monitor as he tracked the progress of his work. The virus was almost complete and tantalizing close to success.

Infuriatingly close.

It merely needed a little more time. Also, Kaiden needed to get his ass in the pod. The killer could almost stab himself over the fact that he'd decided to focus so much on the little bastard. He should have spread his focus and chosen a few different students to keep his options open.

No, that wouldn't have worked, he reminded himself. That might have made it even slower. Kaiden had been in the Animus pod daily, so this was definitely the right thing to do.

If it wasn't for the fact that he'd almost been caught.

That infiltrator of Laurie's had come close to discovering him while he made some reconfigurations. He didn't even have time to play and simply had to eliminate him before he could alert anyone. Gin was only able to stuff him quickly in a storage unit after he'd used his blackout device to create a safe a path through the relevant cameras and sensors. Usually, he wouldn't have minded if they found one of his victims. In fact, it was part of his modus operandi according to his file—very visible victims for the shock value—but not this time.

Too much was at stake to be caught now. He seemed to have bought himself breathing space by assuming Raynor's façade, but this was cutting it close. He would have to leave soon. When his virus exploded, the mainframe would be the first place they checked, even if they didn't quite know what was happening.

Now, he merely had to wait. Only a little longer, he assured himself and reined in his impatience.

Kaiden finished chewing the piece of waffle in his mouth and moved the eggs nervously around on his plate. He needed to make a note to tell Chiyo to not make being late a new habit. Then again, punctuality wasn't his strongest trait, either.

"Are you ready to go, partner?" Chief appeared over his shoulder.

He sipped his coffee and shrugged. "I can't say for sure. I don't really know what we'll have to deal with."

"You got this. Come on, this was your bread and butter at one point," the EI reminded him.

The ace drank the last of his juice. "Oh, I have the run and gun stuff down. It's merely anything else they could throw at me."

"Good morning, Kaiden." The infiltrator slid onto the bench across from him and set her tray and tablet down. "I trust you are prepared for the finals?"

"Mornin', Chiyo. I'm as good as can be." He heard the doubt in his tone and grimaced. "This is probably the most blind I've gone in. I don't suppose you were able to work a little hacker magic and find out what's going down, did ya?"

"I researched a number of previous tests, as I've done for all of them," she assured him as she unwrapped the plasticware. "But I can't say I have much to offer. It's always different for each student. There are some similarities depending on the class, obviously, but for the most part, the map, objectives, enemies, and everything else change out for each student."

"Well, I guess I'll have to stick with as good as can be." He sighed.

"It's not like you to be so unconfident, Kaiden," she said nonchalantly as she poured fruit into her oatmeal. "Do you think you've finally met your match?"

"Me? Nah, not at all," he replied defensively. "I got this. It's what I do, after all. I'm simply admitting that I don't really know what's in store. Plus, this will be the first time I've run a solo mission in a while. Well, besides all the training in the last week."

"Aces are the leaders of the soldiers, right?" Chief interjected. *"I wonder if they will give you AI partners to lead or something."*

"An astute observation, Chief. Nice to see you again." The infiltrator waved at him.

"Howdy, Chiyo. You're looking good this mornin'."

"Salutations, Kaiden and Chief." Kaitō appeared on Chiyo's EI device. *"Best of luck during your test."*

"Hey, Kaitō. Thanks." Chief actually sounded cheerful and earned surprised glances from both Kaiden and Chiyo. *"What? I said I'd get better."*

"Maybe I will have to command a squad of artificial teammates, but I wonder if they would be as good as the teammates I've had. If I gotta tell them what to do every couple minutes, I'd lose my—" Kaiden stopped himself with a cough and sipped his coffee. "But no big deal. Considering the scenarios I've run, I feel confident that I will have no problems in the test."

"They could draw from a pool of unknown enemies. Perhaps they'll have traps and pitfalls. It would make sense for them to create the most difficult maps they can, considering this is for the master rank."

"Well, this ain't the initiate year anymore. Gotta get to the hard stuff eventually, right?" he asked around his last mouthful of eggs.

"You say that so calmly," she noted dryly.

"Your tone seems more dubious," he retorted.

Chiyo brushed it off. "Besides training, did you do anything else to prepare? Have you used your spare Synapse points?"

The ace retrieved his oculars. "I wanted to spread them out on some unused talents. But Chief goaded me into maximizing one that he was interested in and promised that it would be good."

"What talents did you take?" she asked. He nodded to her tablet. Chiyo looked down as the screen changed to his talent tree and the new talents.

EI Mastery: Further upgrades and unlocks specialty abilities of your EI partner.

Status: 3/3

"More upgrades for Chief?" she asked. "I thought you already finished this talent."

"That was Next-Gen. This is a sub-talent that was

JOSHUA ANDERLE & MICHAEL ANDERLE

unlocked when I completely developed that talent. Now, I have a few others to fill out, but my hope is that one of them will upgrade his people skills."

"Pot and kettle, partner," Chief returned smartly.

She nodded and switched her gaze to the trail of students heading to the Animus Center. "You should head over, Kaiden. I've barely started eating and I'll be here for a while. The tests are being run together with the third-year tests, so it's first come, first served. If you hurry, you'll get a good place. They are handing chips out like they did with the Co-op Test."

Kaiden picked his tray up. "I gotcha. Do you want me to sign you in?"

"You know you can't do that."

"Still, I felt I should offer." He tossed his tray and jogged backward for a few steps. "I'll see you in a while." He disappeared quickly into the crowd.

"You know, Chief has become more pleasant," Kaitō ventured.

"What makes you say that?" Chiyo asked as she spread jam on her toast.

"I believe you would call it a vibe?" The Fox EI sounded thoughtful. *"Maybe those upgrades are working."*

As Kaiden flipped the blue chip into the air to signal that he was part of the second group, someone shouted his name.

"Kaiden! Friend Kaiden. Good morning to you." Genos and Jaxon approached.

"Good to see you, Genos." He pocketed the chip and shook the Tsuna's hand. "You too, Jax."

"I wanted to wish you well before the test. Kin Jaxon and I will go in with the first group," Genos explained.

"Do you know if anyone else is in the first round?" he inquired.

"About half of us, with the exception of Julius and our new friends along with Cameron, Raul, and Luke," Jaxon confirmed.

Kaiden nodded. "Chiyo is still eating and the guy who gave me my chip said I just made it, so I guess she'll be in the next group."

"The tests will be completed all in one day, thanks to the expanded wings," the Tsuna ace mentioned.

"That's a nice change from last year—one and done." Kaiden was relieved. The wait was often the worst part.

Jaxon nodded. "Much more efficient, yes." He tapped Genos' shoulder. "We should hurry along. Our tests will begin soon, and we need to report to the pods."

"Best of luck to you." The ace grinned and gave them a thumbs-up. "You guys will do great. Tell the same to the others if you see them."

"You could send them a message before the tests start," Jaxon reminded him,

"Oh, yeah. I guess that's an option, huh?"

"Will you watch from the observatory?" Genos asked.

Kaiden thought about it but only for a moment. "Sure, Genos, and I'll cheer for ya."

"Much obliged, friend. We shall return the favor, as always," the Tsuna promised.

"I always like playing to a crowd. I'll head over there

now." He placed a hand across his chest and pointed two fingers into the air. "Good luck you two."

His friends nodded and returned the salute. "Your form has improved, friend Kaiden," Genos commented approvingly.

"It's one of the things I've practiced. Go on and head in. I'll watch y'all go out there and kick ass."

Genos gave another bow. "Farewell friend, see you soon."

Kaiden chuckled as his friend walked away. "He's got this. What about you?" he asked Jaxon.

"I am well prepared. How about yourself?"

"I got this. We'll all get through it."

The Tsuna nodded. "I shall hold you to that. We shall see you once we finish. Farewell."

As Jaxon walked away, Kaiden left the building and sent out a message of encouragement to his friends beginning the tests and another to the others to meet him at the observatory.

"Raynor, are you there?" Laurie asked into the comms. "Aurora, are you getting anything?"

"Nothing, Professor," Aurora informed him. *"For whatever reason, his comm link is down."*

"You can't even deduce why?" he questioned. "Contact Cyra and tell her to find him and head to the mainframe. We can't have any problems, especially during the testing week."

"Understood."

Laurie sighed and looked at a screen that contained dozens of panels that all displayed the mainframe room. None of them revealed anything at all that might begin to answer his questions.

CHAPTER TWELVE

As Gin watched the tests on the monitor screen, his gaze searched continually for Kaiden, although he knew it was pointless. He would have received a message if the student were among the group

"You can't avoid this forever, kid," he muttered—another pointless exercise. It wasn't like the ace knew what was about to happen, but he needed to vent his frustrations somehow.

He sighed and accepted that this wouldn't be as fun as he'd thought it would be. Once he was done there, he would return to the world and his usual hunting grounds—as in anywhere but there.

It wouldn't be long now—both for how long he would have to wait and how much time he had left before someone noticed something was off. His gut feeling leaned toward the premise that time had all but run out.

The door to the mainframe room opened. *Speak of the devil.*

A woman with long black-and-violet hair entered. "Can

I help you?" he asked crisply but took care to add a little politeness to the businesslike tone.

"Doctor Egon?" Cyra asked, confused. "What are you doing here?"

"Looking over the mainframe during the testing period," he explained with a vague shrug that might suggest anything at all—like he assumed she knew what he meant, which made it less likely that she'd ask more questions than he wanted her to. "I was told one of Laurie's assistants would handle it, but I wanted to have a look before I headed to my post. When I arrived, no one was here."

"Yeah, that's what I'm trying to figure out," she stated. "You haven't seen Raynor at all?"

"Not today, no." Egon folded his arms and assumed a thoughtful expression—not a concerned one because he didn't want to panic her. Merely a little questioning to fit the occasion. "It seems unlike him to avoid his duties."

"No kidding. He almost seems to enjoy his busy work. I can usually pawn off the stuff I don't want to do on him." She chuckled and placed a finger on her lips. "No telling, all right?"

"Certainly," he promised. "I'll keep a watch for now, if you like. You can head back."

"Thanks, but I'll take another look around for Ray," she stated with an undertone of definite irritation.

Gin flinched and his thoughts immediately considered unfolding the blade under his wrist and eliminating her. It wasn't the safe or sensible option, though. He'd already increased the risk of detection when he'd killed Raynor. It was probably only luck and the use of the mod that had allowed him to kill the infiltrator without discovery—and, of course, the fact that Laurie probably wasn't on edge. If he was looking for the man now and had sent this woman to search for him, he'd definitely pay a lot more attention if she vanished.

"Maybe contact his residence?" Egon suggested after a short pause during which he collected his wayward thoughts. "Perhaps he felt under the weather and couldn't make it in today."

"I guess, but he would have sent a message or warned me if that was the case." She sounded sure of that but shrugged. "Thanks for stepping up. I'll put in a good word with the professor—uh, with Laurie."

"Much obliged." He nodded and returned his attention to the monitor. "I'll report back later."

She nodded and left. The killer refocused on the monitor as a few students finished their tests. "Wrap it up, kiddos," he whispered. "I need to crash this charade in a hurry if you please."

"Have you found Raynor yet, Cyra?" Laurie asked over the comm link.

"No, sir, not yet. But you don't have to worry about the Animus. Egon is in oversight there."

"Egon?" the professor questioned. "I thought he was supposed to monitor the central console here."

"He said he stopped by to look in on it before heading there," she explained. "But that Raynor wasn't here when he arrived."

"Even so, I would prefer that he oversee the map

uploads. I'll have to check who's running it now," he muttered. "Strange...I didn't see him on the sensors or the cameras for the mainframe room earlier."

"Maybe he stepped out to answer the call of nature?" she suggested.

Laurie sighed. "There could be a number of reasons and you had to go with the obtuse one." She could almost hear him rolling his eyes. "Continue your search for Raynor. I'll contact his home and send a couple more techs out to look around, but I don't pick anything up. He hasn't signed onto the network since he left last night."

"Don't worry about it, Professor. He'll show up. In fact, I'm sure of it. He'd never simply disappear on us, would he?"

"Huh, smart move." Kaiden leaned back in his chair and folded his arms, and Chiyo chuckled beside him. They were in the observation room from which they watched all their friends currently taking their tests.

A large monitor on the wall in front of them displayed several screens so they were able to watch Genos, Jaxon, Flynn, Marlo, Amber, Izzy, and Silas at the same time. The ace used the tablet on the chair to switch between a screen showing Genos' test and Silas'. "Those two will finish at roughly the same time unless one of them pushes it or the other runs into— Oh, a Zealot droid. That's a nasty bump."

"Hey, Cameron said he's looking for ya," Chief notified him.

"Send him our coordinates," he instructed. "But I doubt

he'll make it unless he is right outside. It looks like Jaxon and Amber are almost done, and the others will probably wrap it up within an hour." Chief disappeared from view.

"Genos has come a long way," Chiyo noted. "He's always been an expert at engineering, but in the combat segments, he's shown that he's both a tactician as well as a warrior."

"Well, considering how he handled himself when we sent him off on personal objectives during missions, the dude has the skills to make a fine soldier as much as an engineer. It's funny to watch him like this and think back to the early days when he was conflicted about following two paths. Look at him now. I guess he learned that you can be as much scholar as a warrior."

"It is nice to see how far he's come," she confirmed and flashed him a teasing look. "Both of you."

"I wasn't gonna say it." He laughed.

"*I detect a lie*," Chief jeered in his head and the ace scowled.

"Not out loud. Give me a break," he said defensively.

Chiyo chuckled and refocused on the screen. "You should head back to the Animus Center soon. Get ready to hand your chip in."

"I'm the only one going in next, huh?" he asked as he stood and stretched.

"I believe so. I have a chip for the next group and considering that the others are even later than I am, I would imagine they will be in the next group or the one after." As she finished talking, the door to the room opened.

"Howdy, how are the games?" Mack asked as the remaining members of the group walked in.

"They were pretty good. I guess you can catch a few minutes of them," Kaiden chided. "Where have you been?"

"Waiting on Mack to finish his third serving," Otto mumbled.

The vanguard held his hands up defensively. "Hey, I wanted to make sure I have the energy for the test. I walk around in heavy armor with a giant cannon. Come on."

"It's all good, Mack. We're here and we're in the third group." Otto sat and kicked his feet up. "Which means we'll kick it here while you two go and do your thing."

"Just me, buddy." The ace thumbed at himself. "Chiyo missed this round. But at least you only have to focus on me. It spares the awkwardness of having to ignore the others."

"You'd better have a hell of a good run for all the smack you're talking right now," Mack challenged.

He smiled as he walked past the group toward the door. "Maybe you haven't noticed because of all the times I've been busy saving your ass…" He turned and saluted. "But I always have a damn good game."

CHAPTER THIRTEEN

The Animus booted up the map with a brilliant white flash that filled his vision for a few seconds. Kaiden landed with a jolt and immediately noted his new location. He was surrounded by jungle with the rush of water as a backtrack somewhere behind him punctuated by... He frowned as he tried to identify what could only be defined as a crackle.

His gaze settled on the smoldering remains of a ship. Pieces of metal spiraled downward as smoke billowed overhead. "Are flaming ships my calling card now?"

"Better than being your epitaph." Chief chuckled.

The ace pushed through the underbrush and inspected the ship. "Do you see anything?"

"Yeah, a downed ship."

"Helpful, smartass," he grumbled. "I mean are there any tech or supplies we can salvage?"

"There are bodies to your left."

"What?" He spun and noticed three bodies on the ground. One was missing a leg, and the trio's armor and helmets had all sustained varying degrees of damage. He knelt beside one who lay face-down, flipped him over, and recoiled when the visor of the helmet fell off to reveal the face within. Although covered in smoke and blood, the features were twisted with terror.

"Lord, what happened to these poor bastards?" The chest of the corpse carried a World Council logo. This was replicated on what was left of the side of the ship's hull, although partially obscured by the smoke. "Do you think this is a reenactment?"

"That's always possible, but you would think that would be a bit tough, even for a final," Chief observed. *"Then again, maybe if it is, they want to see how the mission could have gone if someone actually survived the crash."*

"Can you look it up on the net?" Kaiden asked as he patted the bodies in search of supplies.

"Nope, it's a test, remember? That would constitute cheating."

The ace rolled his eyes as he moved to the second body. "Yeah, because when you're out in the jungle running down a terrorist commander, it would be poor sportsmanship to look up your— *Gah!*" He recoiled and drew Debonair as the body lurched forward and swiped at him. The man wheezed and coughed as he sagged once again, and his chest rose and fell painfully with his ragged breaths. One eye, visible through a crack in his visor, rolled up to look at Kaiden.

"You...finally activated? Good." he wheezed. "The camp is...two clicks south... Give them...a thrashing for us." He took one last breath before his eye fluttered and closed.

"What the hell?" he asked, bewildered. "Activated?"

"That's something of a weird premise." Chief sounded as confused as he felt.

"We have a destination now, I guess." He stood and shook his head. "I'll have to make do with what I have."

"Which is only your guns and a few thermals since they locked your loadout," Chief reminded him.

"Yeah. That's a real pain in the ass, but I guess that's the point."

"Let's get to it. We gotta eliminate the boss and blow the outpost to hell." The EI noticed that he looked around rather wistfully. "What are you lookin' at?"

"I'm taking in the sights, is all," he explained with a shrug. "It reminds me of the Amazon."

"Do you really think they would send you back there so soon?"

"It's been months. I gotta get over it." He holstered Debonair with a decisive motion. "Ready, partner?"

"You bet I—huh?" The EI interrupted himself and his eye scanned around in Kaiden's HUD.

"What's wrong?" the ace asked. He immediately drew his rifle and primed it.

"You didn't see that?"

Kaiden looked around but saw nothing but foliage. "See what?"

Chief's eye narrowed. "Nothin'...I guess."

"Do you think he's catching on?" Sasha asked.

Laurie looked pensively at the screen. "That pilot's last words...he said 'activated.'"

"They both caught that, but I think they believe they are merely in a recreated simulation or didn't pay it any mind."

"Those involved in these projects have explicit instructions not to do or say anything that could create suspicion in those who are undergoing the tests." The professor downed another glass but of water this time. Although he tried to hide it, two of his fingers trembled. His concern was changing to either worry or anger.

"He was dying, so it's not like he could be reprimanded at this point." Sasha sighed. "We're lucky the homunculus was still able to be activated at all. Ironically, they seem to be more durable than their creators."

"Another point for them," Laurie muttered. "All things considered, we are lucky, I suppose. This mission should be rather easy for Kaiden. In fact, I would almost say its cheating in comparison to the other tests."

"Silver linings. We look for them in dark moments."

"Please, keep your poetic musings to yourself," the professor snarked and refilled his glass with a few ice cubes and more water. "I'm better at it anyway."

"I felt it was apropos," the commander said lightly. "I estimate that this should only take Kaiden around two hours to complete."

"Hopefully sooner, considering his talent for wanton destruction." Laurie leaned back and tilted his head as his eyes narrowed. "Assuming nothing goes wrong, he'll do fine. I know it."

"Hurry the hell up!" Gin screamed in his head as the

loading indicator on the screen inched ever closer to one-hundred percent. This was a stupid plan with too many variables and too many chances to get caught. What the hell was he thinking when he put all this together? Zubanz might have been right. He should have simply—

In a flash, the screen went dark. The killer felt a chill of concern but smiled when it reactivated after a second or two. A prompt from the BREW device notified him that the virus was ready, and he looked at Kaiden's picture one last time.

This was a great plan.

―――――――――

Cyra made her way through the plaza toward the tech center to inform the professor personally that she couldn't find or reach Raynor. A call notification popped up onscreen.

"Hello? This is Lead Infiltrator Cyra, how can I—"

"Cyra, this is Officer Duke." Although the man obviously made an effort to remain calm, she detected hints of real fright. "Your partner, Raynor Wilson, is dead."

For a few moments, she froze in stunned shock but shook it off and sprinted to the building. "When did it happen? This morning? Was he sick?"

"No, ma'am, you don't understand. He was killed. We found his body in a storage closet. He's been dead for about a day."

"But Laurie talked to him last night," she protested, her mind racing. "Have you contacted him?"

"Negative. We tried but he didn't answer."

"Dammit. I'll go to him now. You need to inform the directors." She signed out as the doors to the lobby of the tech building slid open and she bolted toward the elevators.

Gin stared at the console, his expression resolute as he inputted his final commands. He walked to the back of it and checked the BREW device. This was it. With a satisfied smile, he pressed the button on the top and the light turned white and then red. It wasn't blood, but the color was at least similar. In the circumstances, it would do.

He resisted the urge to look at the screen one final time as he slid his hands into the pockets of his lab coat and strolled out of the mainframe room. He was passing the Animus level seven hundred halls when a message on his visor confirmed that the virus had now downloaded and activated. The lights above the doors flickered and shut off temporarily, and he smiled.

Gin so badly wanted to revel in the chaos and actually enjoy what he'd unleashed, but he had places to be now.

"Professor!" Cyra shouted as she entered Laurie's domain.

He turned with a startled look. "My word, Cyra, you look like—"

"Raynor is dead."

"*What?*" he shouted, aghast, and both he and Sasha pushed from their chairs. "I just saw him—"

"Last night, I know. I told that to the officer who informed me. He said his body was found in a storage unit. He was killed about a day ago."

"Someone was murdered on campus?" Sasha looked at Laurie, his expression instantly somber. "You don't think—"

"Professor, I read an anomaly from the Animus mainframe," Aurora informed them abruptly.

"What sort of anomaly?" Laurie questioned.

"It doesn't matter, Professor. Egon is in the mainframe and he can deal with it. We have to worry about Raynor's death," Cyra reminded him.

"Egon? I know you said you saw him, but that's not possible. I checked and he hasn't been to work in days. He was on sabbatical," Laurie informed her. "Someone else was scheduled for oversight on the uploads. Are you sure it was him?"

"In the mainframe room—didn't you see us talking on the cams?"

Laurie turned his monitor to show her the screens. "I haven't seen anything. For the last several hours, it's been empty."

Cyra now wore a look of confusion. "I swear, I was there less than an hour ago. He said he would monitor the mainframe since Raynor wasn't there."

"There is a power fluctuation in the Animus Center," Aurora warned. *"The system is crashing."*

"What?" Laurie yelled as he scrambled into his seat and adjusted his monitor. "What is the cause?"

"Unknown at this time, but systems are shutting down and the code has been corrupted," the EI explained.

"The entire code? The Animus code? No one could do something like that so quickly or without attracting notice, not even me."

"Some sort of cyber warfare suite maybe?" Cyra asked as she approached the professor's side.

Sasha raised a finger to the side of his oculars. "Wolfson you need to... Of course you've heard about the murder, but something is also happening at the Animus Center. We don't know yet but get your officers together and send some to the AC for evacuation. Then, comb the island for potential intruders." He signed out and looked at Laurie, his expression cold and serious. "I'll head over there. Let me know what you find when—"

"Sasha, look at Kaiden!" Laurie interjected harshly.

When the commander looked at the screen, the ace was doubled over in pain as the world around him began to disappear.

CHAPTER FOURTEEN

"*K aiden, what's wrong?*" Chief asked as the ace writhed on the ground, grasped his helmet with one hand, and used the other to try to pull it off.

"My head is pounding," he screamed before he finally managed to release the notches and dragged the helmet free. "What's going on? I can't see."

"*There's something wrong with the Animus. The map is disappearing—wait...no, it looks like that's what's happening, but everything is staying as is?*" Chief narrowed his single eye at the outlines of a grid. It appeared that the Animus was powering down but instead of the sky, flora, and ground disappearing, they remained in place. "*If there is some sort of emergency, there should be an automatic desync... Hold on partner, I'll get us...out...of...*"

"Chief?" Kaiden gasped as Chief's avatar flickered in and out on the screen. "Are you okay? Or has my vision gone weird?"

"*I don't...this isn't...normal.*" The EI regained his form after a few minutes during which he faded in and out. "*I've had to increase our sync because something is trying to pull us apart. This isn't normal, Kaiden.*

"No shit," he mumbled. His head felt like it would split at any second. "We need to call this off."

"I don't think that is an option anymore," Chief warned grimly. *"The games are over. We're actually under attack here, Kaiden, and when I look around, I don't think this was ever a game, to be honest."*

Chiyo and the group barreled into the Animus Center as other students raced out. "Which hall was Kaiden in?" Silas asked.

"Five hundred and three," the infiltrator shouted in response. "We need to hurry—use the stairs."

"We'll make way," Mack said as he, Luke, and Marlo forged ahead to shove the retreating students aside so they could make a sprinted ascent.

"What do you think is going on?" Amber asked.

"I have no idea, but Kaiden seemed to be in considerable pain," Izzy huffed as they reached level three.

"It looked similar to the early simulations with the Tsuna," Genos told them. "When nearly all were rejected and couldn't properly sync with the system at first, they would fall to the floor and complain of headaches."

"All the more reason to hurry," Jaxon stated grimly. "If something like that is happening now, with Kaiden showing no previous signs of any issue, something is definitely very wrong."

"There's a tech," Flynn shouted, and the group

descended on the man. "What's gone wrong?" the marksman demanded.

"Hmm? Issues with the Animus," the man explained but sounded rather casual. "But I imagine you've already worked that out for yourselves."

"Why is this not an issue to you?" Luke pushed forward, his tone angry. "This is the first time the system has had a problem in decades."

"It was a good run wasn't it?" he remarked, and his steps didn't slow at all. "If you'll excuse me, I need to report to the tech department and all that."

"Wait!" Chiyo called. "Our friend is still in there. All the other students look like they were ejected but something is wrong with his simulation."

The tech merely smiled blandly. "I'm sure he'll be fine." With a final wave, he turned his back on them and headed down the stairs.

"What the— What a dick," Flynn spat. "Fine, to hell with him. Let's get to the hall."

Gin hurried down the final flight of stairs and turned into the lobby, where a group of security officers escorted students out. He passed them without a backward glance and stepped into the courtyard, a pleased smile on his face as he kept his head slightly lowered so he didn't have to make eye contact with anyone.

That smile, however, turned into an annoyed frown when someone blocked his path.

Commander Sasha stood in his way and seemed to have

done so deliberately.

"Afternoon, Commander. I'm sorry if I seem abrupt but I need to get to the lab. There are problems with the Animus, as I'm sure you've heard."

Sasha scowled, anger evident on his face despite the fact that his eyes were hidden by the oculars. "I have, and I also know you seem to be the one to blame."

"What gives you that idea?" the killer asked but barely made the effort to even try to sound genuine. "And if you're right, do you really want to do this here?" He removed one hand from his pocket, ready to draw Macha sheathed on the back of his waist in an instant.

"What did you do to Raynor?" the commander demanded. "And to the real Egon for that matter?"

"Different executions but the same effect." He shrugged, the gesture off-hand and uncaring. "Although I was in something of a bind with the infiltrator, of course. It happened during a time where I actually cared whether I got caught or not. But it worked out in the end."

A gun barrel pressed against the back of his head. Ignoring the implicit threat, Gin turned with apparent unconcern and smiled at the giant man with a blond, slightly graying beard and a long mane of hair. Several security guards stood behind him. "Officer Wolfson, I presume?" he asked with a smile. "Magellan has told me about you. I suppose I should say 'hi' on his behalf."

"I'll tell him that I'm sorry I took his kill," Wolfson replied, his tone angry and mocking. "Do you have any idea how much of a fool you are for coming here?"

"This time or the first time?" the killer asked and slid his hand from his pocket. The weapons aimed at him primed in response. "I guess the ruse is up at this point, no?" He shrugged, deactivated the Wormwood device, and revealed his face. A confident smirk contrasted with sharp silver eyes, and his close-cut white hair gleamed in the sun. He flicked his other hand to unfold his oculars and place them on his face. "Do you really think this will work? I have a reputation for getting out of nearly impossible situati—"

Wolfson pulled the trigger and a blast collided with Gin's temple, knocked him down, and rolled him across the courtyard. The students nearby who weren't aware of the standoff startled in surprise and stared at the body.

Sasha snapped his attention to his colleague, his expression questioning. "I wasn't gonna waste the chance," the large man muttered and held his hand cannon up as if in explanation.

"Boss, look," another guard shouted. Wolfson and Sasha whirled and gaped as the intruder stood and grinned cheekily. His face should have been shredded from a blast like that, but his smile was still in place, along with a shimmering purple shield around his body.

"Those Adonis cannons have considerable punch," Gin conceded and tapped a finger on the shield around his face. "But my shields are like the wall of Troy." His smile wavered slightly. "Well, that's a bad example, but you don't have a horse so I think—"

"Get out of the way," Wolfson yelled at the crowd. Sasha drew a pistol and primed it while the students sprinted or leapt out of firing range. "Fire! Take him out."

Their target formed a wall of energy to prevent the blasts from reaching him, and the shield grew brighter and

JOSHUA ANDERLE & MICHAEL ANDERLE

brighter. "He's overcharging it," the commander warned. "Cease your fire. It'll explode."

The purple-hued barrier now glowed white. One of the guard's shots struck home and the energy erupted to release a wave of energy that hurled all the officers, students, and Gin back several feet. The intruder, however, simply flipped easily, landed on his feet, and used the opportunity to run.

Wolfson, who had the benefit of his enormous weight to anchor him, slid back a few steps but recovered quicker than the others. "After him!" he bellowed, and he and the commander led the pursuit.

Kaiden's friends gathered around his pod together with several advisors and Head Monitor Zhang. It was the only one unopened.

"Can we force it?" Luke asked.

"No, that would only create more problems," Zhang stated crisply as he studied the screen. "It looks like some kind of virus has infected it, but something like that shouldn't be able to disable or affect the system. We have safeguards and EIs set up to deal with any hacking attempt or network attack."

Chiyo looked over the head monitor's shoulder and her eyes widened. "It's changing—mutating."

"Mutating?" Akello asked. "A computer virus?"

The infiltrator moved closer to the screen and scrutinized the settings and coding. "It's reacting to the Animus code, which is why the system can't force it out or destroy it. What that means is that it's already found a way to defend itself against anything the EIs do to try to counter it, or it moves to a different stage that's unaffected by their attempts."

"How do you deal with something like that?" Otto asked. "What can do that?"

"An experimental device stolen a few weeks ago." A voice answered from behind them, and the group turned as Professor Laurie walked toward them with a cylinder in his hand. "This was the BREW device, created as the cyber equivalent of a doomsday weapon. It gets its name from the fact that it can attach to almost any system and wire itself into it, then create a virus to the user's specifications that infects the system. It's almost foolproof." He dropped it on the floor and walked past the group to the monitor. "Even against everything we have."

"Can we use it to deduce what kind of virus it is and make a countermeasure?" Zhang asked.

"No. Once it is used, all the internal systems shut down and it installs its own OS into the system it infects."

"Then should we shut the mainframe down?"

"If we want to kill Kaiden, that's an option." Laurie sighed. "Even then, it wouldn't expunge it, merely keep it there until we turn it back on. Given that it's in the mainframe, it could simply move itself to a different system if we do that. We would have to shut down everything on the island."

"What about off the island?" Akello asked.

"I've already turned off any devices that would allow it to upload to a device in the city or around the globe.

Fortunately, it doesn't move that quickly, but there's still far too much it could do here."

"What about Kaiden?" Genos asked. "Will he be all right? What happened to him?"

"The BREW device was meant to destroy the Animus system, but it also created a virus to attack him personally," Laurie explained. He shrugged, his face flushed with real anger. "By Gin Sonny."

The entire group stared in shock and some gasped. "He's here?" Julius asked and looked furtively around them. "Where?"

"Sasha, Wolfson, and his officers are tracking him right now," the professor explained. "There's no need to worry. They are not only the best we have, but many of them are the best to have come from the military. They will find him."

"But what about Kaiden?" Chiyo pressed. She glanced at the pod and returned her attention to the screen above that currently displayed nothing but darkness. "Is it too late?"

Laurie sighed. "Honestly, I'm not sure that I can… Wait, what's this?" He scrolled through the screens and his eyes widened as he activated his comm link. "Prep my theater," he commanded someone on the other end before he turned to the head monitor. "Zhang, open the pod."

"But, Professor, if we do that—"

"He's not hooked up to the pod anymore," Laurie stated. "At least not his mind. He's in the Animus itself."

CHAPTER FIFTEEN

"I ...I can't feel my...everything," Kaiden muttered and slumped awkwardly. "Are we still in the Animus?"

"Not for much longer, but we won't be going back," Chief said, exasperated. *"I'm not sure how this will end, partner."*

"Well, shit..." he whispered. His mind had gone from crippling pain to what felt like it had cooked in his head and would spill out from his ears at any moment. "I can't even die with any dignity, only curled up like a drugged-out fetus."

"I'm trying to find out what's going on. It's not only the Animus in general. Something's targeted us specifically. Our link... Wait, what's this?" The EI narrowed his eye before it widened rapidly. *"Kaiden, I think I found a temporary fix."*

"Some sort of workaround in the Animus?" he asked, and a little hope seeped into his voice.

"We aren't in the Animus."

The ace blinked. "My mind might be giving out, but I remember getting in the pod."

"You did—we did—but this isn't the Animus," Chief stated

firmly. *"I can't really explain right now, but this'll give you more time. I'm not sure if it'll save you, though, but I gotta do something."*

"Wait—what?" He placed his hand flat on the ground and tried to push himself up. "Where are you going? What are you doing?"

"I'll tell you on the other side... Or never, depending on whether or not this rips me apart."

"Rips you apart? Chief, don't do anything stupid," he demanded while he continued his attempt to right himself.

"Considering the situation, everything seems more desperate than stupid right now," the EI countered and looked directly into Kaiden's eyes in the visor. *"Best of luck to you, partner."*

His avatar swirled on the screen and Kaiden's vision blurred as the world around him darkened. "Chief?" he ventured into the silence, but the EI vanished and the blackness changed to a bright white.

Wolfson kicked in the warehouse entry door as Gin raced down the middle lane. The giant raised his weapon and fired, but the shot rocketed through the killer and exploded a group of boxes a few yards ahead of him.

"Another damn hologram," the head officer cursed. He pounded a fist into a pillar beside him. "Sasha, I've lost him. Have you had any luck?"

"Negative, but it doesn't surprise me. This little disappearing act has allowed him to roam free this long," Sasha answered. "Any reports from your men?"

"None so far, but I still have all their vitals on screen, so at least they're breathing."

"My guess is he's in hiding. He's probably using a stealth generator or mod of some kind to hide from radar and scans."

"I won't give up. I'll get this bastard today," Wolfson promised. "Coming into our Academy and killing one of our own—he'll pay for that."

"Not to mention whatever he did to the Animus and to Kaiden."

"Kaiden?" Wolfson asked. "What happened to Kaiden?"

"We don't know yet, but whatever virus he put into the system not only shut the Animus down but seemed to target Kaiden specifically."

"What?" the angry man yelled. "He came back only to finish Kaiden off? What kind of crazy fool is he?"

"A dangerous one, but as I said, we aren't sure what exactly he did. Keep your focus on catching him and—a moment, Wolfson." The commander exited the link.

Wolfson adjusted his grip on his cannon and continued deeper into the warehouse. There were innumerable places to hide, but if their quarry had chosen to skulk in there, the previous blast had definitely tipped him off to the fact that he wasn't alone.

"Sir, are you there?" an officer asked over the comms.

"Did you find him?" he asked and peered cautiously around a corner.

"Not yet, sir, but I ran into a tech who told me there was a disturbance in the Academy's barrier—a small hole, apparently."

"A hole? Shit! He's making a run for it." Wolfson swore,

and his mind immediately responded with a plan. "Get some flyers in the sky. I'll get to mine. We will not let him escape."

"Wolfson, I'm back," Sasha advised him curtly. "Kaiden is being moved to Laurie's personal theater and I need to go there to see what's going on. Do you have anything to report?"

"One of my men said there's been a breach in the Academy barrier—a small hole. Gin probably used it to slip away."

"In the barrier? That's supposed to be impenetrable without access to the main terminal."

"And the Animus was supposed to be too, and he found a way around that," Wolfson retorted. "Go and see to the boy. Me and my men will take care of this bastard."

"I'll make sure to send some of the submersible recovery droids. They aren't equipped for combat, but they can locate him if he's trying to stay underwater," Sasha responded. "Good luck and stay safe."

"You make sure Kaiden gets back alive," the giant ordered as he raced from the warehouse to his personal flyer pad. "And when he wakes up—if he wakes up—you promise me you'll tell him what's going on."

"I will."

Kaiden was loaded onto the examination table by two technicians. Laurie activated the medical droids and linked Kaiden's EI implant to his console.

"I'm sorry, students, but you can't come in here," one of

the techs announced and tried to force the group back. "You shouldn't have even made it this far. The professor needs to work."

"No one will tell us what's wrong with Kaiden," Flynn argued, his stance rigid and unyielding. "That BREW thingy only affected the Animus, right? Kaiden's out, so why is he still unconscious?"

"Let them in, Gerald," the professor ordered.

"Sir?"

"It's fine, as long as they stay in the viewing area." He spared them a brief glance. "I understand their concern. I am worried as well."

The tech looked both a little confused and offended for a moment before he nodded and allowed them past and motioned to the viewing area. Chiyo and the others walked into the room and pressed close against the window to make sure they each had a good view. A tube snaked down from above and placed a breathing mask over Kaiden's mouth.

"Kaitō, can you tell me what's going on?" the infiltrator asked.

"It's purely a guess, but it seems the professor is using the bots and devices to stabilize Kaiden's physical condition," the EI informed her.

"He said Kaiden was attacked in the Animus, but that his mind wasn't there anymore. What could he mean?"

"I couldn't say, madame. Even with all the knowledge and sources I can find, this is most unusual."

Genos pounded on the glass while he held a button down beside him. "Professor, I know you are busy trying to help friend Kaiden, but we wish to know if there is any way we can help." His question was broadcast over the intercoms in the exam room.

Laurie looked up and pressed a button on his console. "Not at the moment, no, and before any of you try to say you have medical or technological knowledge that might prove helpful, please refrain from doing so. Keep in mind that our staff—both medical and technological—are some of the top minds in the world and even in other worlds. This isn't that simple a matter."

Chiyo sidled up beside Genos who held the button down as she spoke into a microphone. "You said that his mind itself was in the Animus. What do you mean?"

After a pause, the professor sighed. "I'm not completely sure myself. It would appear his EI was able to sync Kaiden's mind into another aspect of the Animus using a previously activated map. The conscious separation when a student goes into the Animus using one of the pods should be monitored by the pod itself. In this case, however, it's monitored by the Animus system. That should, quite frankly, tear him apart mentally. It's like putting a biological mind into a super-computer."

"Then is he—" She really didn't want to finish the statement.

"I wouldn't do all this merely to have a pretty corpse," Laurie stated caustically. "Like I said, he's alive, even if by unknown means. I don't know how his EI managed this and it shouldn't even be possible for it to do something like this. Even my own wouldn't be able to." He stroked his chin as if in thought. "It might be because of their unique link. In Gin's single-minded desire to destroy Kaiden, he might have chosen the only target who could survive an attack like this. In fact—" He leaned down and tapped on the keyboard at his console to open a pod on the other side of the room. "I have an idea, and one of you might be able to help."

"We'll do anything we can," Jaxon answered without hesitation. "How can we be of service?"

"I said that Kaiden is currently in another map. It's roundabout, but I might be able to establish a link to that map and send someone there to help him."

"Help him? Like pull him out?" Amber asked.

"Not quite, but certainly help him live," the professor explained. "He is currently in a coma, at least in appearance, but the reality is that he's simply not here mentally. The best way I can put this is that the simulation is 'grounding' him mentally. But should he die in there, he will, subconsciously, perceive it as actual death and he will be brain dead. There will be no way to come back from that."

"But if he thinks he's in the Animus, wouldn't he believe that he would restart and be booted out?" Jaxon asked.

"And go where?" Laurie inquired. "Where he is right now isn't particularly stable as it is. The system might try to bring him back, but that could crash his little bubble and the system as a whole, which would lead to the same outcome. Kaiden is capable, but with the stress he's under and the fact that the map seems to be a simulation of some sort of droid factory, he may be overwhelmed." He studied the ace's body thoughtfully. "Which is somewhat fortunate, actually. If he was on a solo map, we wouldn't have this option at all."

"That's the last map we did as a team," Chiyo realized.

"Do you think Chief thought this could happen? That's why he loaded this map instead of one of the training ones Kaiden's used?" Silas wondered.

"Who knows. Right now, we need to get in there and help him," Cameron demanded and pushed his way toward the exit of the viewing area.

"I appreciate the enthusiasm, but two things need to be said first." Laurie cut the excited chatter off. "One, only a single person can go in, as I said. We don't want to have any more trouble with the simulation and right now, it's purely theory until I can open a link." He shrugged. "Although it looks possible, considering that I'm working with what's left of the system, but any more than one would still be too much strain."

"What's the other thing?" Izzy asked.

"You would be in the same predicament as Kaiden," Laurie stated quietly. "If I could simply open a link and pull him out, I would already have done that. This is one possible and temporary interim measure until we fix this, and if you die…" He let the words simmer with the very sobering implication.

This didn't stop any of them. "I'll go!" Flynn offered and stepped forward.

"It should be the best one here. I'll get in there." Cameron placed a hand against the marksman's chest to stop him.

"In that case, shouldn't it be Jaxon?" Marlo asked. "But if we need to protect Kaiden, it should be one of us heavies."

"He's right." Mack pounded his fists together. "This ain't a normal mission. We can't complete the objectives and bounce. It'll be for as long as the professor needs, and we heavies specialize in that."

"It won't be any of you," Laurie announced when he finally had a moment of silence in which to speak. The group looked at him in confusion.

"But you said—" Flynn began before the professor held a hand up and pointed to the side of the room.

The students' eyes widened as Sasha walked past and over to the pod.

CHAPTER SIXTEEN

W olfson started his ship, his expression grim as the engines hummed and the lights in the cabin turned on. "Who's in the air?" he asked over the comms.

"This is Officer Hancock, aboard ship 008."

"Officer Baron, ship 011."

"Officers Sandra Tola and Ron Jetton in ship 003."

"That'll do for now. Wilson, lead the scouting party here at the Academy. I'll send for more ships shortly, but I want this place turned upside down in case this was a ruse," the head officer ordered. "And make sure that all the carriers and vehicles are shut down."

"Acknowledged."

"I'm taking off." He pulled up and his ship was in the air in seconds. "All ships, activate your radars and scanners. Link them to the recovery droids in the water and keep a close watch. Even with a head start, the closest land he can swim to is far enough away that he couldn't have made it there yet, even with all his fancy gadgets. Ship 003, check the southern coastlines. 003 and 008, check the east and west. I'll take north to see if he's trying to wait us out."

"Understood."

"Roger."

"Ship 011? Baron? Do you acknowledge?" The comms remained silent. Wolfson looked hastily at the screens connected to the other ships. 011's blank eyes stared back at him and he cursed vociferously. "Din jävla, idiot! It was a ruse. He's on that ship."

As if in response, the craft banked and hurtled forward to sail over the mountains. "All ships, follow 011," Wolfson ordered as he turned to pursue the stolen vessel. "Shoot it down."

Kaiden awoke to the sounds of metal on metal and a whipping wind. He looked at the sky and then at his body. He was still dressed in his armor and jacket and felt the weight of both Sire and Debonair. "Are we still in the Animus? What's going on, Chief?"

He waited through a few moments of silence.

"Chief?" he finally asked again.

"He doesn't appear to be with you, Kaiden," Laurie's voice answered in his ear.

"Professor?" he inquired, "What's going on?"

"I'll give you an abridged version. Gin Sonny attacked you and the Animus using an advanced corruption device. He tried to use it to destroy your mind while you were in the Animus."

"Gin? Gin is here?" the ace demanded incredulously. "Where? You have to get the others out of here if he's—"

"It's already taken care of. Don't worry about that now. You have to worry about what's going on with you."

He stood awkwardly and rolled his shoulders to ease the stiffness while he scowled at the factory in the distance. "I don't know what's going on. This isn't the map I was on. The last thing I remember is Chief saying he'd found a workaround or something. He said he wasn't sure if it would work, disappeared, and everything changed."

"Well, it worked, but you're still in peril, Kaiden. Somehow, Chief was able to move you from one point in the Animus to another, where the virus couldn't track you. But it's only a delay until we can get you back," Laurie explained.

"So I'm still in danger? It felt like my mind was being cooked."

"In a way, it was. Certainly, I'll have to examine you once the trouble has passed," the professor concurred. "But for now, you cannot die. I know that seems obvious but the mission you are in is active. You will soon have to deal with hostiles who attack you and if you die in the engagement, you will truly die, Kaiden."

"But I'm in the Animus, aren't I?" he pointed out. "I have no plans to lose or anything, but shouldn't the rules still apply?"

The other man sighed with very audible regret. "I've already given the long explanation to your friends. In short? Yes, you are and no, these are obviously not normal circumstances, are they?"

"Right on both counts, I guess," the ace muttered.

Something whirred past him and he spun instinctively, snatched Debonair from its holster, and fired to down an Observer droid. "Dammit, they're onto me already."

"I'm sending you help, but it will take a few more minutes. This is new territory for me and in the field of Animus design."

"You sound like that should be a triumph," he noted sarcastically.

"It should be but trust me when I say I wish that it were under different circumstances," Laurie admitted.

Kaiden followed his instinctual response and jogged toward the factory before he slid to an abrupt halt. It had taken a while to realize that his only objective was to live. He acknowledged that going toward the place that built more killer robots was not the greatest plan. Instead, he turned and hurried off in the other direction.

"Do you know what happened to Chief, Professor?"

"I can't say, Kaiden. What he accomplished here? Honestly, I didn't know it was possible."

"Didn't you design him?" the ace asked as he ran cautiously into the thick forest. "There has to be a graph or something somewhere that explains what's going on with him."

"Chief was designed to grow and evolve, like other EI, but it had fewer limitations. It was connected to you using the EI implant—to your mind—which made it able to think more creatively, more out of the box than a normal EI."

"More like a human, you mean. Less ones and zeros."

"In a sense, but it's still software, and the potential was what I was observing. I still didn't think something like this was possible—to react like it did especially under the circumstances and getting attacked by a potent virus like that. It might be the only reason you are alive."

"He."

"What?"

"Chief is a he. It's weird that you keep calling him it."

"You assigned him that," Laurie pointed out.

"I'll bring it up when he comes back," Kaiden retorted but froze when something crashed through the trees behind him. "Where's that backup?"

"Still on the way. I am trying to load him at a location close to you. While I can get him somewhat close, you'll have to meet up."

"I'll get around to it—and he? You sent one?"

"It was all that was possible given the circumstances. And not to add pressure to you in the middle of a struggle, but he will now suffer the same repercussions as you will."

"So if he dies…"

"It's for good," he finished, his tone grim.

"Who did you send? Dammit, hold on that for a moment." The ace spun and drew Sire to fire a blast behind him that broke the shield of a pursuing Guardian droid. "I didn't realize they could move that fast on treads," he mumbled under his breath, charged another shot, and released it as the enemy responded with two shots of its own. He fell back and the shots went overhead. His blast impacted with the top of the droid a moment later to blow it open and halt the mechanical it in its tracks.

"That can't be the only one," he said quietly and tensed at a rustle in the trees. Moving quietly, he retrieved a thermal from his belt, activated it, and lobbed it into the canopy. It exploded and something spiraled downward along with twigs, leaves, and branches. An Assassin droid, he realized, charged a shot, and fired. The mechanical sprang up, twisted its torso ninety degrees to avoid the shot, raised an arm, and flung a spear.

Kaiden moved his head instinctively, and the weapon pierced the tree alongside him. He raised his rifle to fire back but hesitated when he noticed a line at the end of the haft. The droid pulled back and toppled the tree in an effort to smash him under it. The ace cursed and aimed his rifle. The tree erupted under the barrage and scattered debris in a wide radius. He used the spewed wood and leaves as cover to put some distance between himself and his attacker.

The Assassin droid severed the wire with a blade that ejected from its gauntlet and stalked toward him. He charged another shot and fired but his target leapt out of the way, so he added a second shot that hurled it back into the previous large explosion. Simply being caught in the charge of the blast wouldn't finish it, so he stowed Sire on his back and attacked the mechanical. His plasma blade had heated sufficiently when he vaulted on top of his opponent and dug the heated metal into its head. He gritted his teeth and dragged the weapon down the middle.

Its red eyes powered down and went blank and he heaved a sigh of relief as he scrambled quickly to his feet and drew Sire. He paused when two more droids lumbered toward him. It seemed he was a little slower than usual, but he didn't have time to worry about that. He drew Debonair but before he could even aim, two shots cracked from behind him, whistled barely over his shoulders, and pierced the chests of the approaching mechanicals. Their aim was true and destroyed the power units. The droids teetered for a moment, then toppled heavily.

Kaiden waited as a man in blue and green medium armor approached. The helmet he wore had a visor specifically designed for marksmen.

"Flynn?" he guessed and grinned at his new ally.

The sniper unlocked his helmet with one hand and removed it casually. The ace's eyes widened in surprise. "Sasha?"

"It's good to see you alive and active Kaiden," the commander responded cheerfully as he replaced his helmet.

"You're the one Laurie sent?"

"I volunteered, actually. I came to protect my investment." He raised his rifle and fired three shots to easily eliminate three flying drones that were half a click away. "And to help a fine soldier in a bind."

The ace smiled, held Sire close, and offered his hand. "Thanks. I'm glad we can finally fight side by side."

The commander looked at the hand with a raised eyebrow. "You should keep your hand on your weapon, Kaiden," he said as he stepped past him and vented his rifle. "For now, at least. When this is over, I'll gladly accept your thanks."

CHAPTER SEVENTEEN

Wolfson continued the headlong race after Gin. Ships 003 and 008 had finally caught up and took turns to fire on the stolen vessel. Due to the high speed of the chase and their attempts to not to cause excessive damage to the environment, they hadn't accomplished much.

The head officer, though, constantly tried to argue that allowing the killer to escape would be much worse than a potential forest fire.

He took his own shots when he could, but his quarry—or his EI—was quite proficient at flying the craft and avoided the attacks with ease while barely losing momentum. The giant drew closer and closer in his modified ship, but he didn't feel any elation. He should focus on demolishing the craft. Those barriers and shields of Gin's might be strong, but an explosion and impact like that would shatter them with ease and, hopefully, his body along with them.

The hopefully part of that was what generated the

worry that gnawed at him. It would mean relying on chance. He wanted to be sure this bastard was dead, which meant he would come back with a body—or a head, at least. He was a reasonable man, after all.

Gin's ship dropped to a much lower level, and before Wolfson could follow, it rocketed up quickly and whipped back to fly over him and draw in behind ship 003. "Shit! He's gone on the attack," Wolfson roared. "003, get out of the firing range."

His warning came too late. Two shots from the enemy ship struck to blow their target's engines. The cockpit of the stricken craft opened, two seats ejected, and the officers made it out safely. But their leader's momentary relief was replaced with shock and rage as the attacking ship slowed and lined up on the pods that floated free of the ship.

"He's going after the pods," Wolfson warned and yanked his ship around to intercept.

"I'm on it, sir." Hancock came in from above and fired at the fugitive. Gin was able to spiral away from most of the shots but took two to the hull, while one skimmed the aft engine. The officer danced his craft broadside to ram the enemy vessel. It whirled in a circle, but the pilot used the opportunity to fire through the front of ship 011.

"Hancock!" Wolfson yelled, with no response. The damaged vessel plummeted to crash into the forests below. The giant's fists tightened as he flew over the massive explosion and he grimaced before he set his features into a hard expression as he turned to pursue the stolen and now compromised ship.

He caught up quickly as the damage was enough to

slow it considerably. His aim perfectly centered, he fired, but Gin maneuvered above the shot seconds before it struck and swooped over the head officer's ship. A dull clunk alerted him to an unwelcome passenger.

"Damn fool!" he growled. The killer had fallen onto his ship. He retrieved his hand cannon, expecting the revenant to drop from the ceiling or barrel through the front of the vessel. Instead, the instruments and screens on his dashboard blackened one by one, and the hum of the engines grew quieter. His adversary was deactivating his flyer.

Wolfson knew he didn't have the knowledge or speed to quickly circumvent Gin's actions, but he wouldn't let this end there. He raced to the cabin and snatched a case from the top shelf, used a length of cord as a makeshift strap, and attached it to his back. Armed with a rifle from the gun cabinet, he approached the door, but it wouldn't budge. The giant spat and gripped the emergency lever with both hands.

He grunted with effort as he used much of his strength to force it open. The door fell off and he managed to avoid the quick suction of air that followed. The ground was coming up fast, but he pushed the thought aside, ducked out, and raised his rifle. At a quick flash of white, he fired several shots. They were nothing more than warning shots at this point as he couldn't reach him effectively from his position.

The craft continued to hurtle earthward and was barely above the tallest trees at this point. He removed his hand from the trigger and grasped the rifle by the center, then held onto a railing inside the ship with his free hand. He waited, his eyes squinted at his enemy, and grinned when he wondered who would go first. Finally, the killer bailed from the top of the craft. The giant's grin broadened into smug confidence that suggested predatory anticipation. For all his gadgets and tricks, the man still couldn't make himself a backbone.

The uppermost twigs and leaves scraped against the bottom of his ship, and Wolfson hurled himself out and down to the forest below.

***

"The commander is in, Professor," one of the robots stated.

"Finally. At least something is going right," Laurie replied wearily. "For now, that should buy us more time, but we still need to get dear Kaiden out of there."

"Is there anything I can do?" Chiyo asked. He looked at her in surprise and registered that she was only a few feet away from him.

"I thought I said to stay in the viewing— No, it's fine. I'm simply not used to having so many people in here," he confessed. "At this point in time, I'm still trying to figure out how to get Kaiden back to a point where I can do anything. He's essentially in a weird limbo space within the Animus. I had hoped that bringing him here where I had more control over the Animus systems and a better link that something would come to me. But to be perfectly honest, he might be safer staying there than me fiddling with anything on my end."

"Professor, are you there?" Cyra asked and appeared in a holoscreen above them.

"I am. Report, Cyra."

"I'm sorry, Professor, but I'm locked out of the mainframe proper. There's nothing I can do the normal way."

"You seem to be leading me somewhere," he noted dryly. "Out with it, Cyra. Do you have a suggestion?"

"Using the suite, I might be able to go the more direct route, but I'm not sure that I would be able to stay in very long. Something this complex might make me as much a vegetable as Kaiden is."

"Time and place, infiltrator," Laurie advised as he considered her idea. "We might have to use that, you're right, but don't go in alone. I'll send a few technicians to you."

"Do you think those cyber jocks can keep up with me? Even with more people working on it we won't have a lot of time. I'll need someone experienced so when we can get in, we can identify the problem and get out as quick as possible."

"You are certainly correct, but we don't have many options considering Raynor's passing. The closest infiltrator in my employ is currently in New York and even using my personal transport, that's a forty-minute flight and I can't—"

"I'll go," Chiyo offered. "I'm an experienced infiltrator and I will volunteer. There is no need to worry about legal issues."

"Is that you, Chiyo?" Cyra asked. "That could work, but you have to understand that neither I nor the professor knows what's going on in there. That aside, we also have no idea whether the suite is able to make it into a landscape like the suites normally would. None of the parameters we worked with previously apply here. We could be going into an abyss."

"You're doing this to help Kaiden, right?" she inquired. "My assumption is that you hope that if you can remove the BREW system from there, the Animus can come back online and we can get him out?"

"That is an excellent deduction." Laurie nodded. "Indeed, that is the hope."

"I don't want to simply stand here, then. If I can do something to help, I'll do it."

"Professor?" Cyra asked hesitantly.

"You heard her, Cyra. She'll be on her way." Laurie fixed Chiyo with a half-amused look. "Hurry along, infiltrator. Help bring our boy Kaiden back to us."

CHAPTER EIGHTEEN

"Officers Tola and Jetton, are you there?" Wolfson asked over the comms.

"We're here, sir. We made it." Jetton responded. "Do you want us to converge on your position?"

"Do you have any weapons?"

"We have our pistols, sir."

"Then there's no need to approach. Even with proper arms, there's a good chance it would be a one-sided fight. No offense officer, but this isn't some truant or petty crook." He popped his case open and extracted his armor.

"We don't want you to face him alone, sir," Tola ventured.

"As much as I'm looking for a fight, I'm not enough of an idiot to think this will be easy. So, if you wanna do something for me, listen up." Wolfson donned his helmet and the comm link immediately connected to the radio. "I'll go dark after these commands. I'll send you a message with two contacts who are already on their way. Send them my coordinates and tell them to remain dark until they are within one click of my location. Understood?"

He sent the list to both their inboxes. "Roger. sir. We're on it. Best of luck."

"I didn't get this far only on that," Wolfson whispered, ended the call, and deactivated the link. He'd barely secured his chest plate and arm guards when something rustled a short distance away. Without hesitation, he straightened and fired his rifle. The blast impacted the trunk of a tree and toppled it, and it landed in a flurry of debris and kicked up a large puff of dust.

The aftermath drifted to the forest floor and even coated the giant. The cleaners on his visor wiped it quickly off his screen, and he scanned the area before his attention focused on a moving, human-shaped dust cloud.

"Neat trick," a mocking voice said. Gin decloaked, the left side of his body greyed with dust. "For a second there, I thought you were a lousy shot."

"Even with that, you'd still have an advantage staying cloaked," the head officer observed and turned his whole body to face the killer, his rifle at the ready. "Why come out?"

"I simply want a little fun, Officer," the man confessed and folded his arms. "These last few weeks have been equal parts dull and stressful. My plan was to head back to Seattle after the virus was released and have a grand old time, but you, the commander, and your little guards had to make a big deal of everything."

"You attacked our school," Wolfson challenged. "Took down our systems, murdered Raynor and Hancock—and Egon as well, I assume."

"That would be a safe bet," he admitted. "Although, to be fair, Egon was the only one who needed to die. To keep him as a hostage would have been inconvenient, and he didn't seem like the type to take a payoff." The killer circled the large man as he counted off on his fingers. "As for Raynor, that was simply a classic case of being at the wrong place at the wrong time. And...Hancock, you said? I assume that was the guard who fired at me in the flyer? It speaks for itself, doesn't it?"

"What about Kaiden? Was that some petty revenge on the one who got away?"

"Ah, yes, Kaiden. It's funny how things line up like that, isn't it?" Gin returned thoughtfully. "To be honest, he's the whole reason I came back to this planet at first. Some people want him dead."

"What? Old gang rivals or something?"

The killer laughed in surprise. "He has that many people after him? It wouldn't surprise me. He seems the cocky sort, and it's easy to cross the wrong people with an attitude like that. Trust me, I would know." He shook his head. "No, sir. Do you honestly think any gang would have the creds or ability to interest me? This was some sort of shadow collective. They have big plans from what I assume and have a particular interest in the Academy as a whole. Also Kaiden, interestingly enough, although I think he might merely be a booby prize in the grand scheme of things."

Wolfson was quiet and simply stared at his adversary from behind his helmet. "You don't have any reason to make up such a long-winded story. You prefer to let your actions—your killing—build your story."

"We all have our own technique when it comes to legacy, don't we?"

"Why tell me all this? You don't think they would come after you if they wanted to keep this 'collective' a secret?"

"They can certainly try. My tally has been rather low since I returned, and I could use the numbers." Gin spoke casually and stopped in his tracks. "I don't owe them anything anymore, and I no longer work for them. As for why I bother, would you believe I don't have the chance to have any real conversations? Most people I meet simply try to kill me."

The head officer raised his rifle meaningfully. "You don't think I won't?"

"Despite the fact that you keep calling me a fool, I'm not so stupid that I would believe that." He moved his hand to Macha's hilt. "I don't see therapists that much, but even I have stuff to get off my chest."

"I'll help you with that. I can blow that chest open, and it should relieve a hell of a lot of stress."

"Cute. I can't say I've heard that threat before," Gin lowered his stance and drew his blade out slightly. "I wonder if you can back that up."

They stood motionless, both cold and determined as they stared wordlessly at one another. The killer was the first to move, and he activated his cloak again and dashed at the giant. Wolfson simply aimed his rifle downward and fired, and the force of the blast shoved his attacker into an awkward stumbling lurch. The large man ran forward and crunched the killer aside with the butt of his weapon. He made to follow through with a vicious kick, but his opponent spun and side-stepped the attack. His grin wide, he skimmed the edge of his blade along Wolfson's leg and slashed it across his chest. It dug deep and sliced through the armor.

Rather than back away, Wolfson leaned into the assault. He allowed the tip of the blade to cut across his chest as he moved close enough to grab the man's neck. With a low grunt of effort, he thrust his head into Gin's and rattled him briefly before the killer swung the blade toward his throat. The giant ducked, forced to let go as his adversary brandished his Omni-blade with a plasma cutter and aimed for his hand.

The head officer charged another shot and released it as soon as it was ready. Gin created a quick barrier to stop the attack, but the large man closed again and drove himself through the force of the blast. He pressed a switch on his gauntlet that created a reinforced knuckleduster over his fingers and swung at the other man's head. The killer responded by a violent attempt to grab his arm and flip him. Thankfully, his weight gave Wolfson the strength he needed to stand fast and instead, he whipped his arm back. The force launched the smaller man overhead, and the head officer raised his rifle and fired into the killer's chest as he careened into a nearby tree.

Gin's cloak deactivated as he managed to flip himself and strike the massive trunk with both feet to thrust himself away. He rolled on the ground and stopped on his feet, grimaced, and twisted his neck to the side. "You're fairly quick for a big guy."

"And you're much more durable than I would have thought for an underfed-looking freak," Wolfson snarled.

"Your insults sting." The killer traced a hand across his

chest and the gesture revealed cracks in his armor. "But you've landed some good blows. That last shot pierced my armor's shielding. Not bad. It makes you the sixth person to do that." Gin sheathed both his blades. The giant made no effort to respond and simply ensured that his rifle remained trained on him. "You are definitely a warrior and won't let me get away—like Magellan, but unlike Kaiden."

"Kaiden's as much a warrior as I was," the head officer stated. "He has a natural talent and his skills are some of the best I've seen. It wasn't his responsibility to take you down."

"Perhaps, but if I was one of the first people to put an edge of fear into him, is it not cowardly to leave me on the loose?" Gin questioned. "If we go by codes of honor or morals or whatnot, frankly, I gave up on those a while ago. There isn't much use for them in space."

Wolfson grimaced and fired, and the other man leapt up to land on a branch as his opponent vented his gun. "He's not seen the likes of you, even in his old life."

"I suppose not. It's good to see the Academy finally dealt with that problem within their own ranks," Gin hissed.

"I know your little tragedy—read your profile, actually." Wolfson selected a thermal. "Every soldier has to deal with their first monster. It's what you do afterward that shows your character, and Kaiden kept training and fighting. He would have come after you one day." He activated the grenade and lobbed it at his adversary, who created a shield that blocked the blast but knocked him back to the ground. The killer took a knife from each gauntlet and threw them at Wolfson, who turned his head to the side to dodge one and snatched the other in flight and hurled it away.

"So I'm the one in the wrong? Avenging a fallen comrade? That's evil?" Gin asked. His voice tried to remain neutral, but wrath crept in despite his determination to control it.

"I'm not one to judge the act of revenge. I made plenty of decisions in my career based on that. Sometimes, I'll admit it felt good, and at other times, it cost me even more than before." He closed the vent on his rifle. "But you decided to keep your petty vendetta going and took it out on those who simply tried to do good in the world—in the universe."

"I don't pick and choose, fool," Gin retorted. "You claim to stand for something—soldier, merc, gang member, officer, terrorist—and you wanna test that? I'm happy to oblige." He straightened. "Even the good ones have some gray."

"Is that right?" Wolfson sneered. "You ran away after killing those who killed your friend—the one you took your name from, Gin. You felt remorse then, but you don't anymore, do you? You're merely chasing a thrill, not some nihilistic philosophy."

The killer was silent and stared at the other man, his head angled to the side and his hands clasped behind his back. "This isn't fun anymore."

The giant smiled. "I feel fine."

Gin opened his hands and a flashbang fell. It erupted as Wolfson's visor darkened in response, and when his vision cleared, several Gins sprinted deeper into the forest. *Holograms.*

But his pursuer knew which one was the original, and he wouldn't let him get away.

CHAPTER NINETEEN

K aiden fired two shots from Sire, and both struck the Guardian droid. One ripped its gunnery arm away and the other separated its right thigh from the body. It chunked heavily into a pile of scrap, effectively neutralized.

He vented his weapon and drew Debonair to fire several shots into the droid's chest. With things the way they were, it was better to be sure than have some half-mangled monster creep up and end his options.

"That makes fifteen for me, but who's counting?" He chuckled as he caught up to Sasha and the droid parts and pieces that had piled behind the commander. His eyes narrowed as he frowned and tried to count them in his head. "How many of them?"

"Twenty, including the seven I took out earlier," Sasha advised him and motioned for him to follow. "But who's counting?"

"Mine were bigger," the ace muttered as he fell in behind the commander after one last look at the pile.

155

"You're using a sniper rifle, right? Why are they in a pile like that instead of simply shot through."

"I'm thorough," Sasha stated cryptically. He paused in front of a tree and tapped on it three times. "We're here."

"At a tree?" Kaiden asked, the damage count vanishing as confusion set in. "Is this some sort of secret bomb or something?"

"Secret, yes. Bomb, no." A panel appeared on the tree. "It's good to see that this is still here. This will make survival a little easier." He pressed a few keys and the panel disappeared. "It's open. Only a few more yards."

"What's open?" he asked as he looked back. "The next wave should be on the way soon." He'd barely spoken the words when what sounded like rapid laser fire erupted into the silence. "What the hell?"

"That's likely the turrets I just activated. They should keep them at bay for a few waves," Sasha explained. "But using that terminal also opened a bunker deeper in the forest."

"There's a bunker on this map? It seems out of the way and unnecessary for a retrieval mission."

"This wasn't always for a retrieval mission. The map was used for a survival op back when I was a student." Sasha pointed beyond the trees. "There—that hill. Get over there."

Kaiden nodded and ran forward as the older man brought up the rear to cover him. The ace sprinted to the hill and frowned when he couldn't make out a door or entrance. When he was within several feet of the dune, a shimmer caught his attention a few seconds before a metal door appeared. He grabbed the large latch and pulled, and the door opened slowly. The commander pushed in on his heels and closed the door behind them.

It was pitch black for a moment before several lights illuminated their path down the stairs. They walked down several floors to a holding area with several seats and a table, but more importantly, ammo cases and gun racks.

"I can make do with this," the ace said as he inspected the weapons.

"There seems to be less here than I remember," Sasha noted as he looked around. "I wonder if that is because the map was changed or because you never came here, so Chief had some information missing when he recreated the map."

He froze at the mention of the EI's name. "I wonder what he did, or if the virus was the reason he disappeared," he ventured reluctantly and glanced at his companion. "Do you think he's all right?"

The older man placed his rifle on the table. "I couldn't say, Kaiden. My knowledge of EIs is somewhat limited, even with all my experience and the years I've had with Isaac. All I can offer is that if Laurie doesn't know, I couldn't hazard a guess."

Kaiden sighed as he walked over to the table, placed his pistol on the surface, and sat to kick his legs up beside the weapon. "It's kind of ironic how much I care about the little glow-y bastard now. For most of my first year, I thought I would rip my implant out myself. Now, he's grown on me so much I'm worried I'll lose him because of a mistake."

"It's not your fault, Kaiden. Gin caught us all off-guard," Sasha reminded him. "If the truth be told, I think it was as much Gin's machinations as it was all of us getting too comfortable in this Academy. We thought ourselves safe from intrusion or attack, even though we already had signs of attempts."

"Seriously? When? By who?" he asked curiously. He had honestly thought the Academy nearly impenetrable from anything other than an army. "That shield could probably break diamonds."

"It wasn't only the shield. Our cyber security was better than almost anything, besides a few conglomerates running their own experimental systems and, of course, the WC." Sasha tapped his fingers on the table and sighed. "I should be honest, since we have this time, and I have to confess that I've kept much from you, Kaiden."

"I should let you know that I'm not the best when it comes to touchy-feely stuff. So unless this specifically has to do with me, it's all right if you don't—"

"Those breaches targeted you, as far as we can tell," Sasha revealed. "Do you remember those odd tests you had during your first year? Where you were confronted by Asiton droids?"

"Yeah. I was told those were random simulations that occasionally cropped up as bonuses or to test students." That had made sense at the time and he hadn't questioned them further, although the implications now rapidly became clearer.

"Did you really think we would send Asiton droids after initiates? The droids that caused a two-year long war and took advanced weapons and entire teams of trained soldiers to defeat?" Sasha balked. "No, not at all, but I suppose I should thank you for taking us at our word."

"I guess I'll be more mindful of that from now on," Kaiden replied sarcastically, a little annoyed. "So what's the deal, then? You said someone was targeting me? Why?"

"It's speculation at this point. When you made your first reports, Laurie and I looked into the disturbances and found code in the system that would load those droids at certain intervals. At first, we believed they were put there by a spy or infiltrator, removed them, and locked the system, but it was much deeper than that. We were finally able to purge them before the start of the second year—secretly, of course—with the update."

The ace nodded as his thoughts worked to process what he'd heard. "Do you have any idea who is after me or why?"

"We have speculation, but nothing concrete," the commander admitted. "We believe it to be something called the Arbiter Organization, a rogue sector of the WC. We don't know what their main goal is and aren't sure if they are a real organization or merely a handful of desperate people working toward their own ends. But either way, they seem to have the ability and resources to achieve their goals, at least thus far, and they've taken an interest in our Academy and you."

"It's always the doom clouds that follow me," he grumbled. "I probably shouldn't try my hand at gambling anytime soon."

"Maybe not fiscal gambling, no, but you do seem to do well with the occasional desperate ploy," Sasha sounded upbeat, an attempt to appease the ace.

"That's more skill than anything else. You guys really should have more faith in me, you know," he pointed out.

"You were the one who brought me here after only seeing me fight once."

Sasha closed his eyes for a moment. "I've never told you much about me, have I?"

"No, but you don't seem to tell most people from what I know," Kaiden said. "I thought it was merely the mysterious military commander profile."

The older man undid the locks on his chest plate. "I wasn't always a military man and certainly didn't come from it." He removed the piece of armor and placed it on the floor. "My father was actually a drug runner for a gang in Los Angeles. He cared for us as best he could, but my older brother and I despised what he did. In our youth and stupidity, we ran away to Texas to stay with family and start a gang of our own—one that wouldn't deal with such dark professions. In fact, we would deal with them ourselves, and we would never miss our mark."

Kaiden, who had intended to ask why he was giving him his life story, had his words dry in his throat at the last remark. "Wait, a Texas gang…never miss… You created the Dead-Eyes?"

Sasha slipped two fingers around the neck of his underlay and slid it down to reveal the skull and horns tattoo on his chest. "To be fair, my older brother and a few of his friends have that distinction, but we never really bickered about that too much." He lowered his fingers and leaned back. "I knew about you, even before you came to Seattle. Even when I joined the Academy, I always kept an eye and ear on the gang."

"What made you leave?"

"While we believed our cause was noble, the law is still

always suspicious when it comes to vigilantism—among other things we did to survive." The commander shrugged and gestured vaguely with his hands. "It eventually caught up to me after a bad gig. I wasn't an official merc and we were working on a tip-off. I was caught while the others got away, but my reputation as a gunman was already well known in the area. I was offered two choices—either to come to the Academy with an inflated debt once I finished, or spend around a decade, maybe two, in jail."

He sighed and his gaze drifted to his rifle. "Even with the contract hanging over me, I would be my own free man again in under a decade if I worked things right. Then, life ended up differently than I expected. I already told you I came in as a marksman, then became an ace in my second year, was contracted to the military, and climbed the ranks. When I finished, I decided that I was better suited to helping create the next great soldiers than being one."

"You never wanted to go back?" Kaiden asked. "You could have helped. Maybe if you were there, the gang—"

"My name isn't really Sasha Chevalier," the commander stated quietly. "I changed it because I wanted to get as far away from my roots as possible. It was Cesaro Vega."

"Vega—that means your brother was Galo Vega, then?"

He nodded. "Then you know what happened to him... his passing."

"Yeah, I do... Sorry." Kaiden was genuinely remorseful.

"I've made my peace with it. He would have wanted to go down fighting," Sasha stated. "But it made me realize that the gang life wasn't necessarily long-lived. If I had gone back, it would have been to break the whole thing up. But with our philosophy and how tight-knit everything

JOSHUA ANDERLE & MICHAEL ANDERLE

was, even back then, I knew I would only cause damage. I'm sure most of the members would have carried on no matter what I did, but they would have been separated, which would have only made things harder. So, I decided it was better to be hands-off." He looked at Kaiden with sadness in his eyes. "I guess that only delayed things in the end."

The ace tried to block the memories out. "So I was a pity offering, then?" he questioned. "You heard a member of your old gang was coming by, so you had a chance to make amends?"

"Not entirely. I knew you were coming, yes. I decided to observe you and give you the same offer I had if you proved yourself. As for the fight, you proved that you were a capable fighter and, at the time, something of a punk. But you were at least one with somewhat upstanding values, even if you dealt with them in a rather crass way."

"Oh, I've come so far." He snickered despite the ill mood. "That kid that I helped, was he a plant?"

"No, actually. I was surprised that Hargrove took it upon himself to make the offer. If anything—if my explanation has you doubting yourself—you should take that as a sign that your place here was earned by you alone."

Kaiden thought about it. "Yeah, I guess that does help." They both froze and listened to a rumbling sound above them. "It looks like they made it through the turrets." He grabbed his rifle. "Should we get up there?"

"We could." Sasha shrugged, stood, and walked to a panel on the wall. He tapped a couple of keys, there was another rumble and the sound of laser fire, then everything stilled. "Or I could activate the next line of turrets."

The ace looked at his rifle before he placed it down and kicked his feet up once more. "How many more do we have?"

"This line, one other about one hundred yards along, and a few protecting the bunker itself."

He stretched his arms and folded them behind his head. "Do you have any more stories to share? I ain't got any cards on me."

CHAPTER TWENTY

"Cyra?" Chiyo called as she entered the mainframe room.

"Over here, Chiyo," the professional infiltrator replied. "You made it here fast. I've prepped as much as I can."

She walked over to the main console where Cyra worked off several holoscreens. "What have you found?"

"Not much more than what I said on the call," she explained and turned two of the screens off. "I sent my EI in to try to see if I could create a path for us before we headed in, but it doesn't look like it'll do much good. Even she can't seem to make heads or tails of it. Whatever the device was made with, the program is something unto itself." She closed the remaining screens and shook her head in exasperation. "When we head in, our EIs won't be able to help us all that much, considering that they need to be our link for the suite to work properly so we aren't stuck in a computerized limbo."

"I understand," Chiyo acknowledged and her eyes

glinted with determination. "But I will still join you. For now, this is our best course of action."

"Right, but if this doesn't work, we'll need to abandon the plan or get caught up ourselves. After that, we'll have to think of something else, but it will take much longer."

"That's time Kaiden doesn't have." Her ocular contacts flared to life and glowed in her eyes. "I'm ready to begin."

Cyra nodded and her eyes soon adopted the same glow. "Professor, Chiyo and I are preparing to initiate our suites. I'll try to keep the channel open while we're in there."

"Agreed. When you get your bearings, inform me of what you see. I'll do my best to help you from here, but this is new territory for all of us," he responded.

"Understood." The lead infiltrator nodded before she turned to her companion. "Let's get in there."

The two women focused on the mainframe screen and their bodies stiffened as their tech suites initiated.

When she entered, Chiyo saw nothing but small lights, odd shapes, and emptiness between. She looked down— her first mistake because there was no floor beneath her. Various bizarre lights tumbled or spiraled around the void. "This is…the mainframe?"

"Not exactly." Her companion drifted toward her. "I've been in the mainframe a few times, actually. It usually looks like a giant grid with buildings to represent different functions and system coding floating around. It's actually relaxing given that it's a mental projection of a super-computer." She spun and studied the sight before her grimly. "This is…not so soothing."

"Where do we begin?" Chiyo asked as she looked around. The entire experiment now seemed rather daunting. "I can't see a target that we should be—*agh!*" Both infiltrators clutched their heads as spasms of pain coursed through their minds. Bile stirred, something that Chiyo had never felt even during the most strenuous use of her suite. "Something's wrong."

"Everything is wrong," Cyra muttered and drew deep breaths in an attempt to steady herself. "The suite creates a landscape projection when we use it, so it's easier for our minds to except, but this…I don't know, void is the best it can do. It's harder to accept and we're getting feedback as a result. It'll only get worse the longer we stay in here."

"That's troubling." The student groaned and shook her head. "We really don't have that much time, then."

"Maybe less than I thought," the other woman agreed.

Chiyo floated deeper into the void but found nothing that she could use. "Usually, there's some sort of terminal or object that would be the target of the attack, but I can't see anything like that." She squinted to peer at the lights. "Perhaps we might find something in the lights."

"Maybe, but I'm not sure if we can actually interface with them. I think they are simply there like distant stars," the lead infiltrator surmised. "Let me check in with the professor."

———

"Professor, are you there?"

Laurie continued to observe the screen that displayed Kaiden and Sasha while he attempted to maintain what was left of the Animus system. "I can still hear you, Cyra. What do you see?"

"Darkness and pretty lights—well, maybe not pretty. More like bizarre. But we can't see anything that looks like a nodule or target."

"It may be fairly deep within, depending on security and the scope of the corruption. You may have not been able to get very far when you entered."

"Agreed, but we don't know which way to go. We're not on any normal plane. Chiyo and I are simply floating around in here. Not to mention that we were affected by feedback only a few seconds after we got in here. I'm not sure when the next wave will come and how long we can hold up against it."

The professor grimaced. Everything was simply done as they thought of it, and he'd been too preoccupied to have given this idea much more than hasty initial thought. However, this could turn out worse than even his already significant fears. "Can you send out a scan? Perhaps that could—"

"I just tried. It only scans a few feet ahead and our EIs are using most of their power to keep us stable in here."

Laurie's hand balled into a fist and he uncharacteristically pounded it into the panel beneath him. "And you can't establish a visual link either?"

"No, sir. I'm not sure how you can actually hear me on your end, but I can barely hear you on mine."

He sighed. For the first time in a long while, he was at a loss. He looked at Kaiden on the screen and then at his body on the table. "Dammit," he whispered. "I'm sorry Kaiden, Sasha." His expression bleak, he spoke into his comm link. "Cyra, I don't wish to potentially lose anyone else, so if you can't find anything within the next few minutes, you need to—"

"Hold on, Professor. Chiyo said she sees something."

"What is it?" he asked, and a faint trace of hope returned. Anything was better than the nothing they currently had.

"It's a light of some kind...no, this one is very different." Cyra looked to where Chiyo pointed. What had, at first, seemed to be a small speck of golden light among the multitude of gibberish had now grown in size. No, she realized. It hadn't grown but instead, it moved closer.

The sphere brightened as it rocketed toward them.

Cyra drifted back to move out of its path, but her companion remained in place. "Chiyo, we don't know what that is. You need to get back."

The student simply waited for the orb to career toward her. The lead infiltrator wanted to haul her out of the thing's path, but the light reached her before she could move. She held her breath but there was no impact. Instead, the light stopped and now hovered in front of the girl.

The brightness seemed to dissipate before a line formed and extended far into the distance. Chiyo motioned for Cyra to follow. "Come, this will lead us to our target."

The other woman was shocked. "Did you do something? Do you know what that is?"

Chiyo looked back, her eyes bright again. "I believe so, but what it is right now is our best chance."

CHAPTER TWENTY-ONE

G in slid down the ravine and rolled at the bottom of the hill onto a load of gravel and rocks. The abandoned outpost had possibly been a hunters' lodge or a training ground back when the Academy was a mixture of Animus and practical training. Either way, it would do for now. He needed to make repairs to his cloaking device and armor and possibly energize his shield generator if he could.

He scrambled off the stones and stretched. That big bastard was much quicker than he'd thought and rather limber for a man who looked like a mountain with a beard and appendages. He took a few steps before he studied the hill. Seeing nothing there, he switched to thermal as an extra precaution. Still, there appeared to be nothing there but a few birds overhead. He had lost his pursuer, then.

His journey into the camp took him past a large building a few stories tall. A quick glance through a window revealed that the inside had been ransacked, possibly by scavengers. If that was the case, he wouldn't be able to do much there. At the very least, though, with the few tools he had on him, he could make simple repairs and perhaps get his cloak working again.

At a rustle behind him, he drew Macha and ducked low as he looked at the rocks that had fallen from the pile, probably jostled by his landing. Still, he had underestimated his foe already and wouldn't make the same mistake again so soon. He crept closer, circled the mound, and froze at a quick movement. A shadow was illuminated briefly by the moonlight.

A knife fell into Gin's free hand from his gauntlet and he cast it quickly at the shadow. He heard a shriek, but it certainly wasn't human, and he walked over cautiously. The rabbit twitched with the knife still in its stomach. What a waste. He couldn't even eat it since the blade was coated in poison.

An odd whistling sound like something in motion was followed in the next moment by a sharp prod into his back. He leapt to the side and rolled behind the cover of the tall building. Cloaked by the shadow, he fumbled and managed to pull the object out. The spike was silver with small indentions in it—ornate carvings resembling those you would find in modified Yokai pistols like the one he used to… Wait a minute.

Oh, that clever son of a bitch.

"Get out here, Gin!" Wolfson roared. He had abandoned his stealth now, but it had served him well.

The killer pocketed the spike in one of the compartments on his legs and peeked around the corner. The head officer stood about seventy-five yards away, holding his rifle in one hand and Gin's old pistol in the other.

"Did Kaiden give that to you?" the killer called. "Did you bring it along for poetic justice?"

"I keep it on me because it is a good weapon," the giant retorted and his gaze settled on his adversary's head that peeked out from behind the large building. "One we designed, I should add. I guess it's merely happenstance or karma that it'll help to finish you off."

Gin fumbled behind him to feel his generator. The low buzzing already confirmed that it was damaged. The spike had gone clean through so there would be no energy available. All in all, a damn good shot and he'd admire it more if it wasn't so inconvenient. He unlatched the generator from his suit. It could still serve a purpose for now. "How did you catch up so quickly? Did you see through the holograms with a special setting on your visor?"

"Your holograms may be able to copy anything on your person, but they don't leave a trail or footprints or kick up dust. It's easy to identify the fakes in a forest, even at dusk." Wolfson now stood only a dozen yards or so away and held his rifle ready. "As for catching up, I know these forests better than you ever will. This used to be where I trained my students when I headed up the military training." He held the trigger down to charge a bolt of energy in his barrel. "But don't think that will make me hesitate to destroy it to kill you."

"I like someone who will stand by their convictions." Gin chortled and the head officer heard something buzz from behind the wall. "I'll stand by mine and continue to live." The killer lobbed something at his adversary and Wolfson fired to gouge out a chunk of the corner of the building before he jumped back. The device the killer had thrown exploded in a large white burst. Wolfson slammed a fist against his chest to activate a personal shield as the blast engulfed him.

He was blinded by the light and the energy reading on his visor warned him that the shield wouldn't hold for much longer. Acting instinctively, he brought his arms up, charged through the blast, and pushed out to the other side in the same moment that his shield disintegrated. As the explosion collapsed on itself, it released another burst of energy that struck the large man in the chest and brought him to his knees. He thrust off the ground and forced himself up as he moved his hand to his rifle, then realized he must have dropped it when the explosion detonated. It lay in pieces and he cursed under his breath as he put the Yokai away and drew his hand cannon.

Moving quickly, he made his way to the building and scrambled in through one of the windows. Gin wouldn't risk a cross-country chase at this point. Now, it was cat and mouse. Wolfson paced slowly to check each room. As much as he wanted to simply fire at random, even he knew that to bring the building down would kill him. Worse, he also knew he couldn't be sure it would do the same to his adversary. He was in the killer's domain, and in a cramped, darkened area, he was at a disadvantage.

A stinging pain pierced sharply through his shoulder blade. He grunted and yanked the blade out. The giant spun and fired, struck the wall, and caught a quick glimpse of a foot as the killer bolted into a room. Wolfson lurched in pursuit, flattened himself against the wall beside the door, and jerked forward to fire blindly into the room before he thrust inside. No one was there but a hole in the ceiling led to the next floor. He fired a couple of shots. While it didn't seem like he hit anything, a thump confirmed that Gin was up there.

He wondered if he should pursue. The killer was more agile than he was, and Wolfson's armor was cumbersome in tactics like this. He scowled when a wave of dizziness surged over him and took a step back to steady himself. He hadn't lost that much blood—the knife, dammit!

A pouch on his belt stored a vial of green liquid which he hurriedly retrieved and opened. It was merely a normal healing serum, but it would hopefully keep the worst of the symptoms at bay for a while. He swallowed it hastily, threw the vial aside as he vented his hand cannon, and left the room to find the stairs. They proved easy enough to locate and he paused at the bottom when a message popped up on his visor. "Not now, you damn—" A map displayed as well with a small yellow dot that moved closer to his position.

Wolfson could keep Gin there long enough. He strode forward, closed the vent on his gun, and held it aloft as he ascended to the next floor. Another thump from above suggested that his target planned to lead him to the top. Well, he would meet the challenge. He continued the ascent until they were on the fifth and final floor. His ears strained into the silence for a moment but heard nothing except the wind and insect noises outside. He crept cautiously along the corridor, although his attempt at stealth didn't help much to mute the thud of his armor.

As he looked inside one of the rooms, a crash behind him made him spin instinctively. Broken shards indicated that a jar or cup had broken in the room opposite him.

Three objects pierced his side one after the other and he grunted as he raised his weapon and fired, Gin rolled under the blast and it sailed through the window. He aimed with a Yokai and fired directly at Wolfson's head. The head officer raised an arm to block the spike, although it embedded itself into his arm through the armor.

He yanked the spike out and glared at the killer before he glanced down to where he'd holstered the Yokai. As he suspected, it was now missing.

"I snatched it when I knifed you," Gin said with no prompting. "Usually, those are throwing knives, but you were moving around too much for accuracy. Plus, given how nice you've been, I wanted to be a little more personal." He looked at the pistol. "It has no more rounds, though. Do you think you can spare some?"

"Have these!" Wolfson bellowed and fired a few more shots from his pistol. The killer weaved through them before he ducked out and into one of the other rooms. The giant simply shifted his aim to shoot through the walls, but nothing connected. He was forced to vent his pistol, but as he moved to pursue, his adversary sliced through the ceiling and fell on top of him to slash and stab at him.

The knife entered his left shoulder and an Omni-blade in his adversary's other hand hacked at Wolfson's chest plate. The head officer attempted to dislodge him, but his assailant held firm until he headbutted him. The impact crushed a part of the killer's helmet and cracked both their visors. The large man was able to shove him off and he followed up with a dropkick that booted the smaller man down the hall.

Wolfson knelt and dragged in a few deep breaths as

pieces of his armor fell away. Gin raised his head and laughed as he pushed himself up, then began to twirl his blades. "How much longer can you last?" he taunted. "You may have knocked me around fairly well, but you're losing blood. I still have all of mine." He stopped swinging Macha and pointed it at the officer. "If you still want to keep going, I'm happy to do so as well. But you can't keep up with me in here."

"I agree," the giant grunted as he stood quickly to catch the other man by surprise. "I can't move like you can and don't have anything other than my fists for close range." He removed his helmet and spat a few droplets of blood. "And, of course, I certainly don't have the strength he does."

Gin tilted his head in confusion. "He?" As if in response, something sharp pierced the front of his chest. He glanced down and grimaced at the claws that gripped him from behind. A fierce roar seemed to give voice to Wolfson's broad grin as Raza pushed off the outside of the building with his prey firmly in his grasp.

CHAPTER TWENTY-TWO

Gin and the Sauren struggled for control as they fell. The killer managed to avoid a bite and tried to keep the huge beast's mouth closed by looping an arm around it as he struggled to pry the unyielding grip loose with his blade. Raza broke free of the man's hold and lunged to decapitate him with another wide-mouthed bite. Gin raised his plasma blade to protect his face and briefly halted the assault as he managed to slice into two of the four claws on his right hand. The alien roared in rage and the man twisted to flip them over each other.

Raza landed on his back and the human rolled quickly, but before he could put any distance between him, his enormous foe caught one of his feet when his powerful tail snaked around his ankle. The Sauren stood and spun to careen Gin into the building before he reversed direction and hurled him into a pile of old training equipment beside a rec center building.

Wolfson landed near the Sauren and teetered for a moment before he collapsed. Raza glanced at the three spikes protruding from the man's side and the blood near his mouth and on his shoulder. "You are bleeding, Wolfson," he noted casually.

"Eh, so are you," the man countered with a chuckle. "And you just got here."

"Blood is no sign of dishonor. You know this," Raza huffed. "But you shouldn't lose too much."

"We'll go over the best way to fight later." The giant gasped as he dragged the blades out with one hand while the other retrieved a small wadded patch on his belt. He squeezed it and pushed it into his side, where it expanded and covered the wounds. "Where is he?"

"Our prey is over there," Raza said and knelt with his claws in the dirt. "For now. He will be dead soon."

Gin stood, shook his head, and eased his shoulders. He fumbled to remove his helmet, which had now been so damaged that it was almost useless. "I really am glad I kept this on for a while longer. Imagine my defeat being a bump to the head."

"Instead, it will be by being torn asunder by teeth and claw," Raza threatened and snarled menacingly.

The killer's eyes narrowed at the Sauren. "Wanna explain what the big lizard is doing here?"

"This is Raza, one of the Sauren war chiefs and a delegate to Earth." Wolfson folded his arms. "He's a friend of mine, but this is also personal for him."

"I guess I have managed to piss them off along the way, huh?" Gin sounded thoughtful. "Perhaps they prefer a more personal approach to diplomacy."

"Exactly." The other man nodded as Raza roared and

charged. He responded by throwing a flashbang at the alien's feet.

It detonated but before he could dodge, a claw snatched hold of his arm. "I can still smell you, pest," Raza raged as he pounded the man with his free hand. The killer managed to draw the last of his throwing knives and tried to stab into the burly arm, but the blade simply slid against the tough scales.

Gin quickly wound his legs over the Sauren's arm and pulled taut to stiffen the limb as he reached for a weighted bar. He slammed it into the creature's eye and Raza roared with pain and fury. While the beast didn't release him, the man was given enough slack that he could draw Macha. He flipped the blade quickly and stabbed into his opponent's hand to drag it back. He repeated the process and finally, Raza let go.

Panting, he pushed to his feet, but Wolfson's shadow alerted him, and he moved aside barely in time. A heated blade skimmed off his left vambrace and he scowled at the giant who smiled smugly as he brandished his Omni-blade

"Are you that petty? Get your own," Gin sneered.

"Take it from me," the head officer challenged and launched into another strike. The killer avoided it, seized his arm, and kicked his leg back into his adversary's knee. The large man dropped instantly to his knees and Gin folded his hands together quickly and drove them into the side of Wolfson's head. In almost the same motion, he snatched the hand cannon from his opponent's meaty hand. "I'll simply take your weapon as a trade," he said mockingly and scuttled back as Wolfson tried to sweep his legs out from under him.

The killer fired but Raza pushed in front of the head officer, raised his arms, and absorbed the bulk of the attack. The Sauren howled in pain and fury but didn't weaken. The hand cannon overheated, and Gin stabbed it with Macha and hurled it aside in frustration. The alien retrieved a razor disk from his belt. He held it up and the rim expanded with whirring blades before he launched it at his adversary, who simply stepped to the side. The man smiled, his expression taunting, and the beast raised a claw and motioned at him as if challenging him to attack.

He almost obliged but a whirring sound behind him alerted him. The noise grew louder, and he fell prone a split second before the razor disk careened overhead and into Raza's hand.

"Shit, that's annoying," the man muttered as he scrambled to his feet and retreated. The Sauren grinned and hurled the disc once more. Gin tried to serpentine around it, but the blade was controlled by the alien hunter who simply followed him and directed it with deadly intent. Finally, the killer leapt upward, flipped over the disk, and sliced it with Macha. He positioned his feet to provide maximum strength and at first, it seemed like it wouldn't give. Eventually, however, the blade penetrated the edge and sliced cleanly to cleave it in half.

Raza snarled as he removed the spiked hunter's lance from his belt and unfolded it. Wolfson stepped up beside him with the Omni-blade. The two waited and stared a challenge, but the revenant simply smiled as he removed his left gauntlet to reveal one of his metal arms. He motioned with it for them to attack.

The duo spurred into the offensive. Raza reached him

first and thrust the lance at him, but Gin caught it with his hand and ran his blade along the edge of the staff as he swiped at the beast's mouth. The Sauren, in turn, caught the blade with his teeth, which angered his opponent. Wolfson circled behind with the Omni-blade and attempted to stab their adversary in the head. The killer released the blade handle and used the lance for leverage to spring up. He managed to dodge Wolfson's attack and kick the beast in the throat.

Normally this would barely tickle a Sauren, but the weight and power of the strike combined with the abnormal strength of Gin's artificial legs were enough to make Raza sputter and release the blade. The man caught it as he flipped over the two and turned quickly to slash viciously into Raza's back. The alien roared in pain and fury and retaliated with an attempt to slice him with his claws. The killer finished what he'd started earlier and severed the fingers he'd damaged before. Instead of another hiss or reaction of pain, Raza whipped his hand back and splashed the man's eyes with blood, blinding him. Gin cursed as he stepped away and tried to wipe the blood clear with the back of his blade hand as he pressed a switch on his belt with the other.

The duo immediately went in for the kill as several versions of their adversary appeared. "You won't fool me with such pathetic trickery," Raza bellowed and speared the lance through two of the holograms en route to real one.

"And you won't sneak up on me by yelling like that," he countered and managed to duck as the lance was about to strike. He gripped it securely, tightened his fist around it, and snapped the head off. The killer forced his eyes open and retrieved the head of the lance as Wolfson surged toward him. It was too late to avoid the attack, but he could reciprocate. He twisted enough that the heated blade passed through the side of his torso above his ribs. The pain was immediate, but he gritted his teeth through it and drove the lance into Wolfson's eye.

The head officer yelled in pain, but mostly, it was a wrathful, damning scream. He fell back and yanked the weapon out of his eye. Blood streamed down his face and he glared at his adversary, his face twisted with malice.

It was time to leave. The killer knew he couldn't keep this up and the two monsters definitely wouldn't stop. He fumbled for the last of his grenades—this one a thermal—and activated it. There would be no one-liners or taunts. He simply wanted this to end. His opponents approached determinedly, and he threw it directly ahead of them. When they realized it wasn't another flashbang, they backed away and flung themselves behind cover a split second before the blast erupted. It worked better than Gin had hoped. The explosion rocketed chunks of the buildings in a broad arc. Wolfson was trapped under the rubble as the killer dashed between them during the chaos, snatched his Omni-blade from the ground, and raced toward the cliffs.

"Wolfson!" Raza shouted.

The head officer struggled under the weight of the debris. "Get him! Go, I'll be there," he ordered. The Sauren nodded and roared as he pursued his prey.

Gin vaulted up and began to climb the ravine quickly. A hasty glance confirmed that the alien had eaten up the distance between them. He could definitely climb faster than the human could, but now that he had his Omni-blade once more, he could manage him alone.

But Raza didn't climb after him. Instead, he pounded the base of the cliff with all his considerable power. It shifted ominously. Was he trying to knock him off? The killer glanced up when rocks fell from above and shoved away from the ridge as the stones rumbled and careened down. He retrieved his blades once again and dived at the Sauren. Both blades sank into the beast's shoulders. "If you won't give up, I'll cut your damn arms off," he warned.

The alien grasped his adversary in response. Gin shuddered when his metallic arms begin to buckle. "My arms will grow back," Raza informed him with a vicious hiss. "But your heart will cease forever." The Sauren roared, plucked the man off him, and hurled him at the cliff. Rocks continued their avalanche and piled on top of him.

CHAPTER TWENTY-THREE

"That's the last of our exterior defenses besides those around the door, but they will be breached soon," Sasha informed Kaiden, who had picked up his rifle and now armed himself with any explosives and spare weapons he could fit on his person.

"Do you have any idea what's out there?" the ace asked and tossed an Altair pistol to the commander. "The ground ain't pounding, so I guess the big guy hasn't come for us yet."

"The big guy? Which one in particular?"

"That experimental Goliath thing, remember? I thought you said you ran this before."

Sasha placed the pistol into a compartment on his leg. "Over twenty years ago. Back then, there was no 'experimental Goliath thing.' The waves merely became harder and harder until the time limit ran out or you were overwhelmed."

"Well, that complicates things," Kaiden grumbled. "With

JOSHUA ANDERLE & MICHAEL ANDERLE

how calm you were, I had hoped that you had a plan for when it showed up. You wouldn't happen to secretly be a top-notch hacker, would you?"

"No, nor is Isaac with me currently. So, if this machine should show up, I suggest our plan is to simply run for now."

"That's it?"

"Run really fast, if you would like something more explicit." Sasha turned to Kaiden. "I also think you shouldn't go out there."

"And let you have all the fun?" he snickered. "I'm good, and I feel cramped down here anyway."

"That's not it, Kaiden. I mean you should stay down here while I deal with the droids." The commander walked over to the panel he'd used earlier. "There's one more setting for this bunker—a lockdown. It will shut and lock the door while reinforcing the bunker with shielding. While it won't last forever, it will buy the professor more time to find a way to get you out of here."

"Oh, don't start with that heroic sacrifice bullshit," the ace protested and looked at the ceiling. "Hey, Laurie! Are you there?"

When he received no response, he glanced at his companion. "When have you known Laurie to pass up a chance to babble? I may not know the specifics of what's going on here, but I understand that everything we understand about the Animus is bent over a railing right now. If Laurie had a plan, I'm sure he would have let us know."

"He may simply be preoccupied in executing that plan," the other man pointed out.

188

"Or things are so bad he can't even talk to us," Kaiden countered. "I know that losing one of your students to a virus that infiltrated the great Animus system would be a stain on the Academy's rep or whatever. But as I see it, I at least have a chance to go down fighting, even if it's only in my head, rather than having my brain cooked while I take a nap. I won't simply hole up in here with my fingers crossed while you run the same risk as I do. What the fuck will I say at your funeral? The great Commander Sasha lost his life against a battalion of robots while I shivered underground? Hell no!"

"So you'd rather die for your pride than potentially live for your future?" the commander challenged, the anger evident in his voice a rather unsettling change from its normal easy tone. He retrieved a bastille grenade which was used to trap others in a shield. "I would have hoped that you would have grown out of such foolishness in the time you've been here."

"Call me a fool or whatever makes you think you can guilt me out of this, but didn't you tell me that you wanted to help make the next great soldiers? How will you do that if you're dead?" the ace demanded, and his hand tightened around the barrel of his rifle.

"Do you think I'd rather see another great soldier die because of me?" Sasha retorted.

Kaiden stared at the man, his expression obdurate. "Wolfson told me a story about something like that when it happened to him. About how soldiers all have to deal with their first time facing their mortality and their fears. It's how they move past them that matters, not the fact that they succumbed to it." He picked his helmet up. "I know what it means to put this on and to wield this gun. I've done it nearly all my life, Sasha. Do you think if I was freaked out about something like that, I would have stayed in the soldier division? That I wouldn't have simply run off to find some cushy job in logistics?"

An explosion outside indicated that one of their last defenses had fallen. "I'm not asking to make a suicide run. Maybe you're right and they are almost ready to pull us out of here, but I'll be damned if that's not the case and I was stuck here waiting for them. And if I get out, I want you to come with me. There's no sense in letting you die when I still have questions I want answered."

"Is that the only reason?" the commander asked.

He flipped his helmet and placed it on his head. "Well, also, I don't like having debts, and I already owe you for bringing me here, despite everything." The helmet locked into place and Kaiden threw his rifle up, caught it, and held it against his chest. "If you die for me too, I'll owe you double and wouldn't be able to pay it back." He took one hand off his gun and extended it to the commander. "Besides, I want to see you in action a little more. When's the next time I'll see you get up from behind that desk?"

Sasha looked at the ace's hand, then at his face. His expression was neutral for some time before he sighed and smiled, replaced the bastille grenade, and took Kaiden's hand. "You don't owe me anything. If you live and make a good future for yourself, that's all I require."

"That's something of a contradiction, but I get ya," he responded warmly as another explosion was triggered above ground. "It looks like they're getting restless." He released the commander's hand and moved toward the steps. "Get your gear and let's go. And by the way, the score's reset, so try to keep up."

The two infiltrators followed the golden light through the darkness. Chiyo felt another wave of nausea, but this one was less intense. Perhaps whatever this was—if it was what she thought and hoped it was—it shielded them to some extent.

"What do you think it's leading us to?" Cyra asked. Her companion stopped and looked up. "Chiyo?"

"Look, Cyra," the student said and pointed at what she'd seen. A large orb with what appeared to be wires or tentacles swirling around it glowed a dark-green color. More white and blue lights pulsed within.

"Is that the nodule?" the lead infiltrator asked. "That looks like a mutant, not a device we can interact with."

"It's the only thing I've seen that shows any possibility," the other woman pointed out. The light they'd followed swirled up to it. "We should at least take a look."

"Okay, so maybe it's a little late for this, but do you think it's a trap?" Cyra asked as Chiyo floated toward the corruption.

"I don't believe so. It's not like it hasn't had the chance to stop us or eject us until now."

"I'm worried something worse will happen than merely shut us out," her companion muttered.

"I understand. You may leave if you wish, but I will continue." The student moved closer to the light.

Cyra grimaced. "Like I'll be shown up when this was my idea in the first place," she whispered. "Hold up. I'm coming."

They drifted close to the egg-shaped object and floated around it for a second. "I don't see any way to interface with it," Chiyo said and sounded disappointed.

"Do you think we should fly into it or something?" Cyra asked and studied the module intently.

"Even I think that's inadvisable." The student infiltrator sighed and focused on the guiding light that danced around. "What are you doing?"

The light scooted down toward the center of the node, where it spun and brightened. A large screen appeared, and the infiltrators floated down to it. "It created an opening," Chiyo said in shock. "But this code… This could take ages."

"Professor? Can you still hear me?" Cyra asked.

"Indeed, but faintly. I've lost contact with Sasha and Kaiden already. I feared the worst," Laurie replied.

"We're…in. Well, as far as we can be," she told him. "We're looking at the code, but even with the two of us, I don't think we have the time to undo this ourselves." The dull throbbing pain in her head began again. "Another wave of feedback will reach us soon. Do you have a plan?"

"You said you can see the code?" he asked. "Tell me, are there remnants of the Animus system there?"

"Yeah, bits and pieces, but the virus takes over the system it infects, right, and uses it against itself?"

"Precisely. And you're right that undoing that by hand without the aid of EI would be close to impossible in a short period of time. But I think I know a way to finish this in minutes."

"Seriously? We're all ears."

"It's not simple, but you need to find the area that controls the upload of the Animus systems, then hack in and integrate the BREW device into it," the professor explained.

"What? That would merely give it access to all the systems that it doesn't control already."

"Yes, but by merging it with the system proper, that will allow the security systems to come back online. Essentially, the BREW device would now be a part of the Animus instead of having merely taken it over. The system will override it and adapt the virus into itself as well as reset all the systems to normal functions. That's all we need for now. I'll deal with the rest when this madness is over."

"It's like you're trying to turn cancer into a functioning organ," Cyra protested.

"Desperate times and all that," Laurie countered briskly. "Get to work, and make sure you eject before it's completed the transfer. A sudden switch like that would shatter your connection and, well…"

"Vegetables. Got it." The lead infiltrator nodded and deactivated the link. "Did you get all that?"

"I've already started," Chiyo responded, her face focused and intent as she worked on it.

"Oh, good." Cyra joined her and checked her progress. "I know you said not to worry about traps, but if it asks for clearance or anything like that—"

"Don't bother. It's probably trying to shut you out using

your info," her companion finished. "You taught me that the last time we worked together."

"I'm glad you pick up on that sort of thing so quickly." The lead infiltrator smiled before she gritted her teeth against another wave of pain. This time, her whole body convulsed instead of only her mind. "It's getting worse."

"Yeah… I'm not sure if—" Chiyo frowned as pieces of her chest and legs seemed to fragment. "I can't say I've seen that before."

"It's not a good sign. We gotta finish this asap. The two worked in tandem to rapidly open the proper channels and locate their target. "We only need to open the link and let it in, presumably," Cyra huffed as they worked to undo the safety protocols. "It's ironic that all the security measures we had in place actually caused the system's downfall."

"That's a rather basic hacking technique, is it not?" the student asked.

"In this situation? You'd think it would simply be easier to nuke it." She chuckled as pieces of her avatar floated past. "Open, you stupid thing, before I'm nothing more than a floating head."

They finished a few minutes later and drifted back as everything on the screen began to flash, disappear, change, and reform. Chiyo's heart skipped multiple beats. She wasn't exactly sure what was going on or what would happen. In fact, she had never been this unsure of anything since she began hacking.

"Chiyo, we need to go," Cyra informed her. Most of the lead infiltrator had faded away now, and a hasty glance at her own body confirmed the same reaction.

"What if something goes wrong? I need to stay in case—

Agh!" Another wave rolled over her and Chiyo felt like electricity surged into her through sharpened metal rods. Even the parts now missing manifested the painful effect.

"We'll come back later if we have to, or the professor will be able to fix it, but we can't—" Cyra's voice cut off when the nodule changed color. The weird appendages vanished and the darkness around them began to glow. "The system is changing."

The student, her trembling lips shifting to a small smile, turned to the lead infiltrator. "Let's go. There's someone I need to see."

"Right, gotta get out of here before... Hey, where did that light go?"

Kaiden leaned against a tree and removed his left shoulder pad and gauntlet to free his movement. They were of little use now anyway. A deactivated droid, the top part of its head blown off and with two holes in its chest, sat beside the tree.

He grunted and kicked it and it toppled clumsily onto the dirt.

Sasha walked toward him with a pistol in each hand. "Where's your sniper rifle?" the ace asked.

"I lost it to an Assassin droid's blade. It sliced the stock and barrel off," Sasha explained, irritation in his tone. "The next wave will be here soon. My radar tells me it's a mixture of Havocs and Berserkers."

Kaiden sighed as sweat and blood poured from his brow. The only part of his helmet that remained was the breather and he kept it on to combat the smoke and dust. "I don't think I've fought one of those. It'll be fun to try new things."

"You won't have much time with them. They are self-destructive droids that pursue their target and explode." The commander vented one of the pistols. "Don't let them get close."

"I'm sure those kinds of tactics and strategy got you a commander position," he joked.

"I also lived long enough to get it, so you might want to follow my lead," the older man retorted and turned to face the tree line. "They are here. We need to—" He disappeared, and his weapons clunked onto the ground.

"Sasha?" Kaiden gasped, pushed up, and looked at the place where his companion had stood. "Laurie? Are you there? What happened to Sasha?"

The only reply was the ominous rumble of the approaching robotic horde as metal feet crushed whatever brush remained. Kaiden turned and readied his rifle. He had said he wanted to go out fighting.

Pity it would be alone, though.

He waited, tense and ready, and his attackers finally moved into view. Havoc droids with chain guns and cannons were followed by small rounded droids, spheres that seemed to roll on two elongated tracks on their body with a single red eye in the center. The sightless eyes stared directly at Kaiden. He remained motionless and the enemy made no further movement, despite the fact that their target stood within vision and range.

The ace scowled at them with both caution and confusion until he was distracted by a white light above which ripped through the sky. The odd sight startled him enough that he almost dropped his gun. The luminescence engulfed the entire map quickly and he sneaked another look at his attackers. A familiar light glowed in the eyes of the droids and he grinned and pumped his fist.

Desync Initiated.

CHAPTER TWENTY-FOUR

Wolfson limped up to Raza, who tried to remove Gin's blade from his shoulder. His other arm had been cut too deeply to be of much use. He placed a hand on the Sauren's back and looked at him as he gripped the hilt of the blade. Raza nodded and the giant used what remaining strength he had to rip it out in one swift movement. His friend hissed for a brief moment but quickly silenced himself. When he attempted to hand him the blade, the alien waved him off.

"I thought it was customary for the Sauren to take trophies from successful hunts," the head officer reminded him.

"Only for the lead hunter. This was your quarry, so you deserve that." Raza straightened and his arms hung limply. "It was my foolishness that cost you in this fight."

"Are you talking about the eye?" Wolfson raised a hand to the wound. "Eh, don't trouble yourself. I had grown too careless myself. Honestly, I simply wanted this bastard dead."

"As did I. He has claimed too many innocents, even among the Tsuna and Sauren." He flicked his head to the side. "He deserved a more prolonged punishment, but as long as he troubles us no more, it will suffice."

"I won't argue with that." The man sat on the ground and studied the ornate blade. "Thanks for coming so quickly. I guess I was lucky you were so impatient that you couldn't even wait for me to swing by and fetch you from the embassy."

"If I wasn't, did you plan to walk back to your home?" Raza questioned, his expression a little sarcastic. "Your subordinates told me you were knocked out of the sky."

"I guess so. I would have made it, too, although you weren't the only one I asked them to hail," Wolfson informed him and winced when his eye pulsed with pain. "I'll need a while to adjust to this." He glowered at the pile of rocks under which Gin was buried. "It's a pity he didn't make it. Sasha told me he was after this bastard for many years. I guess he can take the corpse."

"You have no desire for it?" the Sauren asked in surprise.

"The Academy would frown about a rotting head over my desk." Wolfson chuckled. "He might let you claim it, considering you were the one who finally killed him."

A blue blade pierced a rock in the rubble and sliced through it with ease. "You have to be shitting me." The head officer growled his displeasure as he stood, a little unsteady on his feet.

The rock separated and Gin crawled out, his armor dented, cracked, and broken in places. He used another rock to hold himself up as he stumbled warily down the debris. When he reached the bottom, he fixed his adversaries with a hard look. Blood dripped from his brow and one eye remained shut, and he definitely wasn't smiling. He pointed the Omni-blade at Raza. "Fuck you, gecko." he snapped before he turned his attention to Wolfson. "How's the eye?"

The giant gritted his teeth and stepped forward, but his companion raised one of his weakened arms to hold him back. He glared at him with both anger and surprise, and the Sauren flared his nostrils and nodded. The head officer immediately grasped his intention.

"So, no more fight in you," Gin chided. "Well, it's only to be expected that you would be at a disadvantage. Your depth perception must be shit now."

"Keep talking. The only fight you have left is running your mouth," the other man mocked.

The killer responded by twirling his blade. "You have no armor left—not that it would help much against a plasma blade, of course." He glanced at Raza. "And it looks like your buddy has a couple of useless appendages now."

"I can still rend you with my teeth," the Sauren countered.

"I'm sure you'd give it your best attempt." Gin chuckled. "This fight has been a fun distraction, I'll admit, but I've also known that it has no point." He placed a hand dramatically against his chest. "I've actually been the victor since well before we began. Your Academy is no longer the safe little haven that pumps out the next generation of heroes. Even if you fix the system, do you think the truth won't get out? I've left more than simply a virus during my little visit.

Three bodies so far, as you said. And I'll make it five if you try to continue this."

"You have a lot of empty talk for a man who tried to run away a few minutes ago," Wolfson remarked.

"Like you don't know anything about a tactical retreat," the revenant countered.

"I never was much good at that." He nodded at Raza and shrugged. "He can attest to that."

The killer tilted his head to regard them with open amusement as he swung his Omni-blade and rolled the hilt in his hands. "So then, this is a matter of justice? Revenge?"

"We look after our own, murderer," the head officer stated defiantly. "You won't mess with our students and friends and simply walk away. I don't give a damn how the universe sees you or how you see yourself. You should have known better than to come back here."

Gin was silent for a moment before he grinned. There was an aloofness to it like he was happy despite something, not because of it. "It's a pity your predecessors weren't so hardened back when I was there. Maybe things would have turned out differently if they didn't allow any jackass with an upper-crust background in."

"Everyone has to deal with pain, loss, and hardship, but not everyone turns out like you." Wolfson's expression was grim as he punctuated his statement with a spit of blood.

The revenant's grin faded and for a moment, he remained silent and simply stared at them. "Which one of you has my blade? I'm fairly sure I left it inside the lizard, but it doesn't seem to be there anymore."

The head officer held it up and flicked it casually to the ground a few feet in front of him. "Come and take it."

Gin eyed the blade and took a few steps towards it. The duo tensed, ready for a final battle, but their opponent's eye began to glow. "What? You're still active? I thought I shut you off," Gin muttered audibly.

"Is he talking to himself now?" Raza asked.

"I think it's an EI," Wolfson guessed as something vibrated in his pocket. He retrieved his tablet. The screen was cracked, and the body scuffed, but it was still mostly functional. "Keep an eye on him for a second."

"Of course."

Wolfson opened a message. It was only a few words, but they were enough to bring him relief and joy.

"What? The device destroyed?" Gin shouted in rage and shock. "Nullified—whatever, semantics. They shouldn't have been able to do that so quickly... Damn it!" He drew a small EI device from the back compartment of his armor, threw it down, and crushed it under his foot. "Damn it... damn it!" he roared furiously, and he literally trembled with anger. Wolfson tossed the tablet toward him and it landed at his feet. The killer glanced at him before he picked it up and read the message on the screen.

Kaiden is alive and in recovery.

~ Laurie

The head officer expected this to send Gin over the edge and hopefully spur him to attack in one last attempt to accomplish something. But instead, his body trembled once more before he threw his head back and laughed into the night sky.

"It appears we may win two battles here," Raza muttered as the killer continued to cackle. "One physical and the other mental."

The revenant's laughter slowed. "Smartass." He sighed and chuckled once or twice. "I guess I was never meant for this mastermind crap. I was better off doing what I usually do. Honestly, I should have stabbed him in his sleep—I told myself that a few times, actually." He shook his head. "Even I have to admit, that guy Kaiden is pretty strong too."

Wolfson straightened and fixed him with a hard look. "He also had people looking after him. It wasn't only about stopping you, Gin, it was about keeping him safe."

"That's a nice thought. Do you wanna twist it around about how I'm scum one more time?" he asked and gestured lazily at the duo as if to give them leave to do so.

"There's no point. It's not like you'll remember it when you're dead," the giant replied.

"So you still think you can kill me? I already said that I have plenty left. You're at the end." He held his Omni-blade up. "Do you want one last try at killing me?"

"Damn straight I do," he confirmed. "But it seems it wasn't my fate to kill you." He fixed the killer with a hard look before he and Raza stepped aside. "Only to get you in place."

Gin frowned with momentary confusion before he caught sight of another figure behind them. The man was dressed in black and held something in his hands. The revenant's eyes widened in recognition. He glanced at Macha as he considered the possibility of a swift attack that might reach his two adversaries in time. Instead, he smiled, opened his arms, and dropped his blade.

Three shots entered his chest and exited through his back.

He landed hard and immediately coughed and clutched

his chest. He focused on the pair of boots as they strolled closer, then blinked a few times and smiled at the familiar face.

"Hello, Magellan."

The bounty hunter looked down, his face expressionless. "Goodbye Gin."

"No speech? Nothing clever after all this time?" the killer asked. He sounded disappointed, his voice much shallower, but his smile never wavered. Magellan said nothing and merely studied him impassively. Gin's vision began to darken.

"Funny, all this began with the death of a friend," he said with a weak cough. "And a different kind of friend ends it." He gazed into the distance in the direction of the Academy. A flash of recognition flitted briefly in his eye before his smile vanished to be replaced by a look of sorrow. "Sorry, Gin, didn't listen." With one final breath, his body stiffened, and the revenant was no more.

CHAPTER TWENTY-FIVE

In a darkened lodge nestled in a forest in England, a bloodied body lay face-down on a table, her meal half eaten and her unclosed eyes wide with realization and fear. A man leaned against the doorframe of the main entrance, studied the gory scene, and sighed before his voice hitched in a stifled chuckle.

"I never thought you would go out so mundanely, Adela. Honestly, I always thought you would be one of those melodramatic, crying-to-the-moon types. You always dressed like you were headed to a ball only you were invited to. I really thought you would be slightly more entertaining."

He approached the corpse and flipped it. The body rolled heavily, and he unlatched a silver necklace and grimaced as he lifted it from the pools of red beneath her.

"Well, damn, those little nanos really do a number, don't they? They are great for a silent kill, but they certainly don't leave a pretty corpse, do they?" He snickered.

Unsurprisingly, the corpse did not respond.

"I didn't bring any flowers with me, but I can give you one last parting gift. A proper cremation." He stood, drew a red handkerchief from his vest pocket, and used it to shroud the necklace. Meticulously, he folded the handkerchief and slid it back into his pocket before he walked out of the lodge. As soon as he stepped out the front door, he pressed a button on the device in his pocket and the building erupted in flame behind him. He walked down the path deeper into the forest as the conflagration began to engulf the trees and flora around him. Unperturbed, his pace measured and calm, he took his oculars out and selected a contact.

"Good evening, good sir, it's Dario. I felt I should be the one to inform you of our dear Adela's passing. No surprise? Really, that seems a little harsh, I think, even if you were the one to order it. She could be a little snappy, but she played her part well. I always thought you had a soft spot for a good performance... Well yes, her babbling was a problem, but I still think she could have... Oh, really? Already replaced? And her funds? Oh, well, good for us."

The blaze grew larger and now consumed the forest at a rapid rate. Dario Salvo frowned as he adjusted the angle of his oculars.

"Yes, I understand. However...what? Yeah, it's a little loud over here. I can't really hear you. Oh, fine, ruin my fun."

He held a device up and pressed it and, in a few moments, his cloaked craft hovered above him. A button on his belt launched him to the ship and he activated his EI on the computer.

"Good evening, master. Was it a success?"

"Indeed it was, Falco. Please take me to the home in Manila. I have a call."

"At once, sir."

Dario sat in the lounge of his ship. "There you go. Better? You know me. Causing a calamity is my way of having fun. Well, yes, a blaze in a private area does indeed have a way of making itself known." He poured himself a glass of wine. "I'm not back-talking, merely pointing out the flaws. The nanos did their job but do you really think that wouldn't be suspicious? They already are? Who's they? Well then, more fun for us—or me, if you're too busy.

"Although I have to say, it has been too long since you and I have simply enjoyed a night on the town. You'll be caught up in the busywork of all this." He kicked his feet up and smiled. "I think, if you intend to continue with your role of shadowy overlord, I should find someone else to keep me company. How about that Gin fellow? I know he killed Zubanz, but I never liked him and that means there is a spot open. He seems to be the right kind of... Oh, he's dead? He was alive an hour ago. That fast, huh?"

In the distance, alarms blared, and several patrol flyers rocketed past his craft, none the wiser. Dario took another sip as the man on the other end told him of Gin's fate.

"Well, damn, that's a waste. Double-teamed by a Scandinavian giant and a Sauren—saucy!" He chuckled and fell silent as he listened. "I see. Well, can we use that BREW device for something else? Integrated with the system? How does that work? It still sounds like it could be of use— a little tricky, of course, but I like a challenge. I'll think of something soon. I'm not patient. You know that about me."

He activated a screen to view the flames and plumes of

smoke behind that now faded into the distance, quite beautiful against the twilight sky.

"So, shall I see you at the den tomorrow night? Going out? Where to? Ah, found another problem person, did you? See, you still have the feeling in you. Well, have fun on my behalf. When you get back, I'd like to discuss what we shall do about our little friends at the Academy. My guess is that they will redouble their efforts and even those two V's on the board won't be much help. And with the attack, the security will certainly step up. I'm dying to see if the boy is actually worth all the trouble. I still say that if we simply kill him outright, we can find a way to reset the device… Yes, yes, that's a non-starter for now. Think of the mission. I'll head off and will see you next time you come in."

He put his oculars away in his pocket and a warped smile curled along his lips. He would be patient for now, but he knew that there would be plenty of time and opportunity for him to entertain himself quite soon. And the Academy would make for the perfect place to have some fun.

Kaiden awoke with a start. His first tentative glance revealed that he was in a white room with a window surrounded by white curtains. To his left was a long window that opened onto an outer corridor. He was alone in the room and could see or hear nothing other than the wind and birds outside.

At first, he wondered if this was some kind of death

state and it surprised him that the afterlife looked quite dull. He hadn't expected that. Finally, it dawned on him that this was one of the private rooms in the medbay. He shuffled awkwardly to the side of the bed, swung his feet to the floor, and sat up. The last thing he remembered was desyncing but that obviously meant he made it out. The sky had opened, and the droids had Chief's eye.

Chief!

"Chief! Are you there?" Kaiden called looked around for his oculars. "Partner, did you make it through?"

For a brief second, the ace was crestfallen at the lack of response. That changed when he heard the high-pitched laughter.

"Did you really get all worked up like that over little old me?" Chief asked as he appeared beside him. He, in turn, swatted at the orb and his hand passed right through. *"Watch the eye!"*

"Dick. That was a piss-poor joke there. I actually thought you'd been ghosted," he chided. "What happened to you?"

"Oh, all kinds of shenanigans happened after that virus dropped," the EI stated.

"How did you pull me out?" Kaiden ran a hand through his hair. "Also, did you have to put me on the map with a battalion of bots determined to kill me?"

"Eh, I wanted to give you something familiar to work off," he explained. *"Although honestly, it was the first one that came to mind. I couldn't rely on the single person sims because of the variables. As for how I did it...well, I run back through the scenarios and I can't say I have the foggiest idea."*

JOSHUA ANDERLE & MICHAEL ANDERLE

"That doesn't seem right. I thought EIs had eidetic memories."

"It's called a storage drive," Chief clarified with exaggerated patience.

"Whatever. Was that you who took over the bots at the end there?"

"Yeah, after I helped Chiyo crack the Animus open, I was able to find you, establish a link, and pull you out," he explained.

"Help Chiyo—you can do that too?" The ace leaned back with his hands on the bed to support his weight. "Man, those upgrades really helped out quite a bit, didn't they?"

The EI's eye glowered. *"Seriously? You think that's what let me do all that?"*

"Hey, unless you have a better idea, that's all I can think of," he responded with a shrug.

"It seems to me like you're trying to find a way to say you're secretly the hero here," Chief accused.

"Aren't I usually?" He let the statement hang in the air as the door to his room opened and Sasha walked in.

"Good morning, Kaiden. I'm pleased to see you up again." The commander closed the door. "How are you feeling?"

"Fairly good, especially compared to the other times I've been here. How long have I been out?"

"A few days. You were in a medically-induced coma for a while. The desync was successful, but we had to deal with the mental toll it all took and which still affected your physical health. We had to be sure everything was in order before you became conscious again," Sasha explained.

"In layman's terms, they wanted to fix everything before potentially breaking something else," Chief joked.

"It's good to see you back as well, Chief, and it appears your link was reestablished," Sasha said dryly.

"Yes, sir, I'm feeling dandy."

"For once, I'm glad I can hear him in my head." Kaiden chuckled. "It's an odd feeling, though, and I'm not sure I like it."

"How nice of you," the EI grumbled and rolled his eye. *"See what happens the next time a serial killer turns your virtual world into a smart bomb."*

The ace's face fell before his eyes filled with a look of defiance. "Gin—where is he?" he demanded and looked at the commander.

Sasha removed a box from his coat. "Dead, but this will explain more." He handed the box to Kaiden.

"Dead? Gin's gone? Who got him?" he asked.

"I think you should look into the box. Someone wanted to explain it to you themselves," Sasha said and tapped his chest. "But before that, I want to make an offer on behalf of the Academy, considering the circumstances."

Kaiden placed the box on the foot of the bed and gave the older man his full attention. "And what's that?"

"Considering everything that happened and everything you went through specifically, the Academy will allow all students the opportunity to leave with no debt accrued," the commander explained. "Part of our promise to students is their safety while they are within these walls. We have failed at that, not to mention the temporary loss of the Animus—something we thought was defended beyond approach. As we have broken one promise, we will uphold another. If you feel that we cannot provide for you after you have given your all on our behalf, there is no need to—"

"Spare the business speak." The ace sighed, rolled his neck, and held one hand over his ear as if the conversation was hurting him. "I get the picture, and no, I won't leave."

Sasha looked at him squarely. "Are you sure? This offer will stand until the new year begins so you have time to think it—"

"Hey, remember Gin? The now dead guy who did this in the first place? Remember how he absolutely fucked me up the first time we fought—while I was with other guys, no less?"

"Yes, Kaiden, I am quite aware of who Gin was," he said with some exasperation.

"What would I do if I ran into another one like that? What would I have done if I was attacked like I was and I didn't have Chief, Laurie, or you looking after me—or Chiyo for that matter? Apparently, she hacked into the Animus herself or something?"

"With assistance from one of Laurie's personal infiltrators, yes."

"And me. Don't forget that, partner," Chief interjected.

"Sure, you didn't keep your school's promise or whatever. But the fact is, like you said, I have a future to look forward to now and friends whom I won't abandon after all this. The best way I can create said future is to remain right here. I ain't gonna let a now literal ghost run me out," he vowed and held the older man's gaze unwaveringly.

Sasha nodded and a sense of pride welled in him. He saluted the ace before he turned to the door. "Well said,

Adva Jericho. I look forward to seeing you next year as a master-class student."

"And I'll be a victor soon enough," Kaiden promised and saluted in return.

"I know that you will, but you should know this as well." The commander turned to face him once more. "Your future is truly yours now." With that, Sasha left the room and strolled down the hall. His tablet vibrated and he and took it out to see a message from Chief.

Thanks for stopping by and not telling Kaiden about the Project Orson stuff like you, Laurie, and I agreed. I'll let him know personally when the time is right, but for now, he has enough stuff to deal with and all the secrets and shadowy spy junk are your fields. You keep up your end and figure out this Arbiter Organization thing and I'll look after my partner. And tell Laurie to quit badgering me. I'm sure Kaiden and I will be around soon.

-Chief

P.S. Don't worry, he won't find this message unless you leave it on the desk when he visits. See you around, commander.

He sighed. While he didn't like keeping anything from Kaiden, especially after their heart to heart, he would leave this in the EI's hands. He seemed to have finally grown accustomed to his partner.

In a way, he was almost exactly like him.

After a moment, Kaiden opened the box. Inside was a

tablet and a knife in a sheath. He drew the blade and his eyes widened when he recognized immediately that it was Gin's. The design on the metal confirmed it. He sheathed it and placed it on the bed before he turned the tablet on.

Magellan appeared on the screen. "Hello, Kaiden. I recorded this message as I wanted to let you know myself that Gin is, in fact, dead. I put the three bullets in him myself and watched him stop breathing. Although I can only take credit for the final shots. Your teacher Officer Wolfson and his Sauren friend were the ones who did most of the damage."

"Wolfson and Raza? Man, he'll hang that over my head till I'm gone," he muttered and chuckled quietly.

"I also turned in the bounty and watched as they immolated Gin's body. He's definitely gone. If it feels that I have gone into too much detail, it's because I have to keep reminding myself that he's finally dead. There will always be plenty of assholes in this universe, but I can certainly say that I breathe a little easier now that he's no longer among them."

"Agreed." Kaiden nodded fervently.

"Speaking of the bounty, considering how you were roped into this mess, I felt I should do right by you. I had the commander make contact and sent some creds his way."

"Some extra creds are certainly always helpful," he mused. "If nothing else, I can pay for headache relief pills for all the—"

"...so you no longer have a contract to the academy—"

"Wait, what now?" He rewound the message.

"...some creds his way. They will pay off your debt to

the Academy, which means you no longer have a contract with them. You can and should still attend, but once you graduate, you are no longer bound to any company that could have potentially bought you for however many years. You can decide where to go when the time comes."

Startled, the ace set the tablet on the bed and thought through the implications as the message continued. "I hope you recover quickly, and I'm sorry you had to go through all that. But it's done and you are free of him, and your future's open." The bounty hunter shrugged. "And for what it's worth, if you want to get into bounty hunting when you are done, I know your training as an ace and all. But you seem to be a fast learner, so feel free to contact me. Sasha has my info. Be well, Kaiden. Signing out."

He moved the tablet to the nightstand and considered Magellan's words and the fact that he no longer had a contract. His plan for the next couple of years had been to earn what he could to pay that off but now, he didn't have to worry about it. He could finish his studies and do whatever he wanted.

Of course, he didn't have much of a plan right now—at least nothing other than that one possibility, but that might be tougher than simply earning the creds to buy himself out. But if he could, he would be able to bring along—

"So what's next, partner?" Chief interrupted. *"You have two more years to figure your life out."*

"I can't say I'll ever figure that out one-hundred percent," Kaiden remarked honestly.

"Eh, maybe I was a little too hopeful."

"But I might have something. I'll run it by you when I get it all together."

"Give me a taste. I could help you work it out," the EI suggested.

He mulled it over but before he could begin his explanation, a racket ensued outside as familiar voices asked for him by name.

"It looks like the party is here."

"I guess so, and I'll probably catch hell for almost dying again," he said with a comedic eye-roll. "Like it's my fault or something."

"They are a touchy bunch, but they care, right?"

Kaiden shrugged, leaned back, and waited for his friends to join him. "They certainly do, and I wouldn't change that for anything."

The door burst open as the group entered.

"Back here again, huh?" Cameron snickered.

"Are you all right, friend Kaiden?" Genos asked and ambled to his bedside.

"I'm doing fine, guys, thanks, and sorry for worrying you."

"It's not like you asked for this," Marlo pointed out.

"I heard you fought with the commander inside some kind of Animus mission inside an Animus mission—or something like that," Izzy stated and sounded a little vague about the details, which wasn't surprising. "What happened in there?"

"I'm not sure of the specifics, but it was basically what you said. I was able to survive thanks to the commander and professor." He glanced at Chiyo who lingered in the corner of the room. "I heard I also have you to thank as well."

"And Cyra. It was her plan, to begin with," she said,

walked over, and sat on the bed. "I'm glad I could help and that you are okay."

"Much better than the whole brain-melting thing," Kaiden agreed.

"So, will you take the get out of the Academy free card?" Flynn asked.

"Are any of you?" he asked.

"Well, none of us had a psycho gunning for us and we've all come this far." Silas shrugged. "I'd feel more of a failure leaving now than actually flunking."

"Same here," Julius agreed.

"Like my mom would let me." Amber rolled her eyes dramatically. "Did you know she named a potent healing serum after you?"

"I use it a lot," he confessed. "What about the rest of you?"

Everyone confirmed that they would stay and Kaiden nodded. "I already told Sasha I wouldn't let Gin have the last laugh. I'll stick around."

"Good on ya, mate." Flynn bumped his fist against his shoulder.

"Someone's gonna have to try real hard to get rid of the Nexus crew," Mack declared and elicited giggles and strange looks from the others. "What? Not a good name?"

"Not the best." The ace chuckled and he gazed encompassed Chief and his friends. "But I agree. If someone comes for us, we'll take them on. I ain't gonna settle."

RAZA - THE BROTHERHOOD OF TWO WARRIORS

CHAPTER ONE

Ran'ama Aboren Zin'til Arcquini, the tribal leader of the Tul'Zera Sauren and one of nineteen war chiefs, looked out from the balcony of his spire and over the planet of Saura, his home.

Or it should be, at least, but it seemed he spent less and less time there as he aged. That wasn't abnormal for the Sauren, however, once they earned their marks. Warriors and war chiefs spent many cycles out on the hunt to bring back trophies, valuables. and honor for themselves and their people. But once he'd been elected to both positions two decades earlier, those years of wanderlust should naturally have been brought to a close. However, between his duty as a delegate and his own personal missions, he seemed to be off-world more than he had ever been before.

"War chief?" Raza turned as Ken'ra, his advisor, entered his chambers. "You seem preoccupied."

"I'm merely enjoying a last look upon the land, Ken'ra. I'll depart soon and I wanted to soak it in before my prolonged leave." He turned to face his advisor and friend. "What do you need from me?"

Ken'ra placed a fist against his chest and bowed his head. "It's actually not a request of mine, but from a number of the potential Jah-Wai. They begin their hunt soon, but once they heard that you would not be here to see them off, they all agreed to begin their preparations early so that you could attend."

"The Jah-Wai? Has this cycle's initiation begun already?" he muttered as he shook his head. "They should know not to take it so lightly and that they need that time to prepare. Forsaking adequate preparation simply to ensure my presence is not a sound strategy."

"Agreed, War Chief, but you know the youth. They did not grow up in the thick of blood and battle as we did. As a result, they hold onto traditions with a kind of sacred mysticism rather than as the real trials of hunters."

Raza sighed and descended the steps. "I leave tomorrow days. When do they believe they can be ready?"

His aide looked solemn. "They say they are ready now, sir. We can begin at dawn."

"The only thing more deadly than a fool is an eager one." He sighed again and clicked his teeth in irritation. "But I admire their spirit, and it has been some time since I took part in the send-off ceremony."

"Not since the initiation four cycles ago."

"That long?" he asked, almost aghast. "Very well. I shall meet you at the grounds at the break of morning."

"Very good, Chief. I shall tell them at once. I'm sure they will be ecstatic."

"After the ceremony, I will make my departure, but I

will try to make it back to greet and congratulate the survivors." His aide nodded and departed, and Raza watched his old friend for a moment before he walked over to his chambers. Above his resting mat was a collection of his trophies, the skulls or taxidermied parts of many prey along with weapons and emblems from battles long before. Above all of them hung something that looked out of place —a simple staff, the tip partially broken.

The war chief clawed at the strap on his left arm and unwound it. He moved a finger to trace along a scar there —a curved design with a slash through the middle—and two smaller ones above and beneath it. This was his mark of a successful Jah-Wai, a proven Sauren hunter and survivor.

It took him back to before his duties and life as a leader, to when he was still an unproven little drek. One who believed he was unstoppable, that simply being a Sauren was enough to prove his superiority. It had taken a brush with death against a creature that nature had intended to be a near-perfect killer to prove him wrong and correct his course.

Raza landed with a loud thud, and Lok and Ken'ra eyed him warily.

"We are in the Jearo section of the jungle, Ran'ama," Lok warned. "These beasts will not be the easy prey we have faced before. They specialized in ambush and have claimed Sauren lives before."

"Let them come," Raza challenged and snapped his teeth

as he patted the razor disk on his belt. "We are more than prepared, or did you not come here for victory?"

"Victory is all we seek," Ken'ra attested. "But we would have to return breathing for that to matter."

"Pah, this will be where we make our stand," he stated and gestured into the forest. "When we claim the heads of these beasts, we shall return as Jah-Wai. Then, our true lives can begin."

"You say that, and yet you brought along a memento of your youngling days?" Ken'ra asked and pointed to the training spear on the back of Raza's waist.

He chuckled. "I brought it to throw into the flames at the ascension as the final marker of my youth." He squinted into the jungle. "But first, we need to find our prey before we can fell it and claim our marks."

"If we do this right, that is how this will play out." Lok nodded. "But the Jearo are creatures of amazing speed and their shells are hard to crack, even with our weapons."

"And their poison is lethal to almost any creature," Ken'ra added cautiously.

"Except for the Sauren," Raza boasted. "They cannot poison us enough to kill us, not with our regeneration and blood cleansing."

"It's potent enough to slow our natural healing and clot our blood," Lok reminded him. "If we are stuck, the tide turns to favor them. They could finish us off at their leisure."

Raza huffed air out of his nostrils and pushed past his comrades. "Then I suggest not getting stuck."

The two Saurens shrugged. Ken'ra activated his wrist-blade and followed. Lok held his spear up and with one last look around, trailed behind the others.

None of them were aware of the eyes that studied them intently.

Raza activated his wrist blade and cut through the brush. It was both noisy and inefficient, but he hoped it would draw their quarry to them. He looked back when one of his partners sniffed the air. "Do you smell something, Ken'ra?"

The green-and-brown Sauren nodded. "Yes, but it's familiar." He hissed slightly with a sharp intake of breath. "Blood—Sauren blood."

Lok peered apprehensively into the undergrowth as Raza narrowed his eyes. "Lead us to it."

With Ken'ra on point, the three sprinted ahead and they made their way to a clearing in the jungle. They halted abruptly at the sight of the source of the blood. "Yal'ko and Core..." Ken'ra sputtered, unable to look away from the bodies of their fellow Jah-Wai hopefuls.

Raza approached the corpses to roll Core's black-and-blue scaled body. Three large gashes scored his chest and his tail was severed at the tip. "These are long marks and deep—he was run through," he noted and dipped a claw into the wound. "His blood is thick, like mud."

"Jearo poison," Lok confirmed, and he studied the bodies grimly. "They are mostly intact and look at the way they were gored—Core from the back so the poison set in quickly. Yal'ko's throat was cut, which cut off her air and she could not heal quickly enough to recover."

"They were attacked unawares—an ambush," Ken'ra finished.

Raza eased the body down gently. "Core was an excellent hunter." He glanced at their other fallen comrade, her brown scales darkened by blood. "Yal'ko had almost no equal among our group as a tracker. If they could not pursue the Jearo without attracting its attention—"

"Then perhaps your open defiance was an ill tactical choice?" Lok jeered.

He looked over his shoulder at his sarcastic friend. "I intended to say that stealth has no use in this situation." His eyes widened as he caught sight of something that tried to blend into the jungle as it crept closer to Lok. Raza snatched his razor disk and flung it over the other hunter's shoulder. Both his companions turned as the disk struck the creature, which uttered a high-pitched wail when one of its limbs was cleanly severed. It sounded more surprised or annoyed than pained, though.

The hunters huddled together and focused on the creature as it pushed from the brush. It was tall with a hardened green carapace and stared at them with three eyes in a triangular shape, gray in color with intersecting grids across them. The large mandibles flinched and extended. Its three remaining arms ended in scythe-like blades. Despite that its legs were unnaturally arched, it moved almost like it glided across the jungle floor.

This was, without a doubt, the Jearo.

While Ken'ra and Lok simply stared at it, wide-eyed, Raza smiled. "We have found our prey." He extended one hand and drew it back to call the razor disk back to him. Hopefully, it would slice through the creature's midsection on its return. "It will soon be our prize."

One of the creature's arms turned backward to an unnatural one hundred and eighty degrees. It cleaved effortlessly through the returning disk, shocking all three of its adversaries. The beast released a low, ghastly hiss as it stooped in preparation to attack. Raza held his arm with the wrist blade up as Ken'ra and Lok readied to fight.

"We must find a way to break through its shell," Lok stated. He scrabbled at his belt and tossed a kinetic hammer to Raza. "Our blades alone won't be able to cut through it. We must expose the meat underneath."

Raza activated the hammer and swung it in the air. "I will make sure that happens." He pointed at the insectoid. "Hear me, Jearo. I am Ran'ama Aboren Zin'til Arcquini of the Tul'Zera tribe. I will be your hunter."

Whether the creature could understand him or not, it had enough instinct to know a threat. It leapt forward and Lok and Ken'ra ran to the sides as Raza met it head-on. One of its arms slashed at him, and he blocked the attack with his blade as he pounded its chest with the hammer. The blow pushed the Jearo back, but no cracks appeared. Ken'ra threw his razor disk at the creature. It struck it squarely in the chest but bounced off and careened past Raza's head, who ducked frantically to avoid the bladed weapon.

"My disk did nothing," Ken'ra shouted in surprise.

"But mine did," Raza noted with some bewilderment. His gaze shifted to the insectoid's arm and the fleshy string around the area he had cut, which was unarmored like the rest of its body. He also noticed that the string seemed to tie itself together. Color returned slowly as if something was reforming. He had thought that the Sauren had the best regeneration ability in the galaxy, but the Jearo was proving him wrong.

"We must kill it quickly," he shouted to his companions. "It's already repairing its arm and it can outlast us."

"Continue to strike its shell, Raza," Lok instructed and dashed forward. "I will get you an opening. Build up the force of the hammer."

Raza hefted the weapon and tightened both hands on the haft before he barreled after Lok. The Jearo brought down two of its arms, which Lok blocked with his spear. It readied the third to bisect the hunter, but he held the staff with one hand and raised his other with the wrist blade activated and caught the second strike. He struggled against the strength of the creature. "Ran'ama."

"I'm here," Raza shouted. He stepped past Lok and swung the hammer into the Jearo's side. When it connected, he pressed the switch and the hammer exploded with a wave of force. The impact thrust both Sauren and Jearo back and also demolished sections of the jungle around them. Raza and Lok scrambled quickly to their feet, but so did their adversary. It immediately lashed out at Lok and opened a deep gash in his chest.

"Lok," Raza shouted as the hunter staggered back.

"Raza!" the third Sauren yelled and threw him a vial. "Heal Lok. I will distract the beast."

Ken'ra hurtled in and swiped at the monster with his wrist blade as his fellow hunter caught the vial. Raza ran to Lok, who had already collapsed. He undid the top of the serum and applied the liquid to the wound. "Will this help with the poison?"

"I thought you believed us indestructible." Lok chuckled but without any real mirth.

"You joke now when you're injured?" Raza mocked.

"I'll live. That wasn't enough to fell me," the wounded warrior stated. "But even with the medicine, I am too injured to assist other than as a distraction."

"We may not always see things the same when it comes to the ways of the hunter, but I will not throw your life away. I wanted to fell this beast on my own as it was."

"Hopefully it doesn't come to—"

"*Grah!*" They looked up, their expressions grim. The Jearo had sliced Ken'ra's bladed arm off. He staggered back and his adversary pressed the attack and raised its arms to deliver a final blow. Lok sat hastily and fired a bolt from his gauntlet to pierce the top eye of the beast with an arrow.

"At least we know that is vulnerable," he muttered. "Ken'ra, retreat!"

"It looks like I'll have my wish." Raza stood with his blade at the ready. "You two need to leave."

"You would claim this beast alone?" Ken'ra asked as he applied a gel hastily to his severed arm to stem the bleeding. "The poison that coats its blades is lethal. I can already feel it coursing through me."

"Which is why you need to recover and prepare," he pointed out.

"You think tactically now?" Lok asked.

"You said you would be its hunter," Ken'ra reminded him.

"I am," Raza agreed. "But it might have companions, and I'm sure you don't desire more battle."

The two injured Saurens exchanged a quick glance. "Hunt well, Raza." Ken'ra offered his hand to help Lok to his feet.

"I will." Raza shifted his stance as the Jearo focused its attention on him. "But it will be a short hunt."

The creature wailed defiance and Raza roared in return and charged. He caught an attacking blade with one claw and sliced the vulnerable area of the arm with his wrist-blade. The limb severed easily but his opponent did not ease its assault. It raised a leg and kicked the Sauren back while the vicious blade clashed with Raza's to break it apart and drive him back even further.

Once he recovered, he looked up and snapped at the beast as it waved its remaining arms at him threateningly. A quick glance confirmed that his last attack with the hammer had cracked the creature's armor, but the hole was too small for his wrist-blades. He wasn't sure his claws were long enough to penetrate and damage the beast deeply enough.

As it approached menacingly, Raza's hand skimmed across his old spear. It was small and meant for a youngling's hands and height, but it was sharp with barbed edges on the tip and could be exactly what he needed. He drew and unfolded it, then readied himself as the Jearo careened toward him, its blades poised and ready to run him through.

He held the spear aloft, dug his feet into the ground as he met the attack, and swung the spear to thrust it through the crack in the shell. It slid in easily and skewered the beast. This time, the wail definitely sounded pained.

Raza grimaced at a sudden searing pain in his stomach. The arm he had severed with the razor disk had regrown enough to inflict a deep incision. The Jearo stepped forward and shoved the blade deeper. The Sauren met its gaze boldly and roared at the beast. He snapped its head between his teeth, thrust the spear deeper, and twisted it as he tried to crush its head at the same time. In response, his adversary slashed the hand that blocked its blades, and Raza hissed in pain. He eased his grip enough for the Jearo to twist its head out of his mouth and pull back to free its blades. It dragged them back and flung them forward in a powerful motion. The hunter held the spear firmly and pulled as he moved out of reach of the strike and eased himself off the blade still protruding from his abdomen. The tip of the spear snapped as he yanked it out, and the jagged edges gouged the creature's flesh as it withdrew.

The beast made garbled sounds as it stumbled back. He knew, though, that it could recover rapidly. This wouldn't be enough to end it. Raza dropped the spear and approached the beast. It tried to attack, but the thrusts were slow. He was easily able to dodge some, and others missed him completely. A hard kick brought the Jearo down and he placed his hands on the sides of its head. He summoned all his remaining strength and increased the relentless pressure. Finally, when he was sure he could no longer endure, green blood and clear fluids burst from the creature's eyes and the skull caved inward. The beast went still, and he dropped the head with a grunt of triumph. He was victorious.

Raza stood, looked at the Jearo's blood on his claws, and

used it to paint the Jah-Wei symbol onto his arm. He would receive the real mark—a scar given to those who passed their trial—when he returned, but for now, he simply flung a final look at his prey before he roared into the sky. He was a hunter.

CHAPTER TWO

Raza walked out into the field, surrounded by Tul'Zera Jah-Wai hopefuls. They looked at him in awe as he was dressed in the full armaments of a war chief —a metallic chest plate, three silver rings along his tail, ornaments on his hands and claws, along with a spiked headdress of bone, leather, jewels, and carapace, marked with symbols the Sauren used as emblems of different quarry and hunts. All his impressive attire displayed his achievements.

He stood in the center of the younglings and raised a claw to quiet them. "Today, you begin your trials to become Jah-Wei," he began, and the large ceremonial fire blazed behind him. "Those who survive and return will be seen as younglings no more, but as hunters, brethren to all who also hold the title. You continue the lineage of our race. We are more than simply soldiers, bounty hunters, and mercenaries. We are Sauren, the fiercest race of the known galaxy, and should we discover more, you will be there to show that we will always hold that title."

Roars erupted all around and tails and feet pounded the ground. "And we are Tul'Zera. We are the ones who brought our world together. We are the ones who brought our race to the stars and to the worlds beyond so that our hunt could be everlasting. You have a birthright, but it is not simply given. It must be earned. You must prove what it means to be Tul'Zera."

More roars of approval followed, and the area grew steadily wilder as the blood of the Sauren boiled in excitement. "You have your tasks, younglings, and I hope this is the last time I will call anyone on this field that." Raza looked around, drew his ornate spear and unfolded it, then held it up. "When you return, I will be here. We will honor the fallen and celebrate the victors, the new cycle of hunters. For the might of the Tul'Zera!"

"For the honor of the Sauren," the crowd finished. Almost as one, the younglings departed and raced past each other. Some headed out to the most dangerous parts of the planet, while others would board ships for other planets where their prey waited. Raza watched them go, constricted his spear, and replaced it on his belt. He removed his headdress as the last of them left.

"I'm not much one for grand speeches, Ken'ra." He sighed as his friend approached.

"You still do them well, Ran'ama," he assured him. "Your ship awaits."

"My thanks." He handed him the headdress. "Watch over our people for me until my return."

"Of course, as always." Ken'ra studied the headdress thoughtfully. "At times, it feels so long ago, but I remember when you got most of these markings."

"Most of them I still recall fondly." He frowned slightly. "Others...hmm. If it wasn't a rule, I would wipe them from my collection."

"That's almost heresy," his friend chided and focused on the spines of one of the crowns. "Although I suppose I know what you speak of, which brings me to a new development."

"What is that?" Raza asked.

"Some of the Tsuna delegates wished to depart with you to the embassy," his advisor informed him.

Raza gave him a quizzical look. "Don't they have their own vessel?"

"Yes, but that is currently back on their homeworld, Abisalo, to bring another group to Saura. The trip was expected to be a few days longer, but something came up and one of their ambassadors is needed to attend a meeting," Ken'ra explained. "I can tell them that the use of your vessel is not possible or—"

"It is fine but tell them to meet me there quickly. I'll depart soon."

"Understood, War Chief." His aide nodded and retreated quickly from the ceremonial ground. Raza took another look at the sky before he went to change into his normal attire.

Onboard his ship, he walked along one of the long corridors to the main chamber. This was the Spear of Saura, the first vessel ever built capable of space travel by the Sauren and specifically the Tul'Zera. That had been over two hundred years before and it was now the personal carrier for the tribal leader. It was due for an upgrade, he thought, as the power core was still fueled by energy extracted from Asta crystal, an ingenious idea implemented by Tul'Zera creationists at the time. Now, however, it was only good for long-term space flight as it didn't allow a vehicle to achieve any significant speed and power had to be diverted if they wanted to activate their shields or use more powerful weapons on board.

Then again, the only other species that were currently capable of space travel were their allies, so perhaps it did allow for some leeway.

Raza opened the doors to the gathering area. Inside were two Sauren delegates and five Tsuna—two guards, two delegates, and their ambassador. They turned and the Sauren bowed to their leader while the Tsuna saluted.

"Greetings, War Chief," the ambassador intoned, her voice soft but respectful over the translator. "I am one of the Tsuna ambassadors of the Oiro Clan. We specialize in politics and delegation among the races."

"I assume that duty is relatively new for your clan," he commented. "I don't believe we have met properly. How should I address you?"

She dropped her salute. "I have designated myself Azure after a human word for the shade of the color blue."

"That is fitting, certainly," he noted and studied the ambassador briefly. The female Tsuna were similar to their male counterparts but with noticeable differences—their skin shades seemed more on the lighter spectrum and instead of the seaweed-like hair, they had long fins or tendrils that spiraled out and more ovular eyes, said to give them better sight in the dark. The ambassador was a very bright shade of teal with one long tendril that encompassed her head and fell down her back. "Azure, you seem quite young for an ambassador to other races. What brings you here?"

"Duty, sir, but as you mentioned, communing with other races is a new endeavor for our clan. I was among the first Tsuna born after first-contact and among the first of our kind trained specifically for this position," she explained. "We only met other races a short while ago, of course, starting with you and then the Mirus, followed by the humans."

"I remember. I was among the team that initially discovered Abisalo," Raza recalled and immediately caught himself. "I...regret what followed after that."

The ambassador raised a hand to her mouth and wondered briefly if she shouldn't have mentioned that but recovered quickly. "I did not mean to imply anything, War Chief. The past is done, and we have made great strides since then."

He nodded and immediately recalled one of the symbols one his headdress—one that was inked blue and showed a curved arch with a circle on the front, their symbol for the Tsuna. He was one of the few to have one.

"So, why is the runt with us again?" Jok'sa asked. The veteran hunter scowled at Raza on the back of the transport. "This is Rekka—ritual combat. This is for the rights to this fishy scum's planet. I was told only the best would represent the Sauren."

"Ran'ama deserves his place here," Seeb stated unequivocally and looked the dark-green-scaled hunter in his good eye. "I want to know who let the disgraced bastard in who lost his eye on a simple skinning mission."

Jok'sa growled his annoyance and stood. For a moment, it seemed that he would lunge at the elder orange Sauren, who bared his teeth at his hostility.

"Enough, save it for the fight," Tiox roared and both backed down. "Maybe I'll get lucky and both of you will die and give me a peaceful trip home."

"This old fool is acting like my question isn't well-founded." Jok'sa hawked and spat disgustedly. "All here are veterans, hunt leaders, Ken-Wai, Sur-Wai, and you're a war chief," he said and pointed at Tiox. "Except for him. He only completed his Jah-Wai trial four cycles ago."

"And Ran'ama has shown himself to be the best among his cycle," Seeb stated.

"You show bias for one of your tribe," Jok'sa responded dismissively.

"He has proven himself, having already taken on a Ken-Wai-level hunt on his own," Tiox stated. "But more importantly, he was among the group that discovered this planet. As a member of that team, he has hunter's rights along with the others. As Rekka only allows for eleven members at most, he was chosen as the representative."

Jok'sa eyed Raza again. "Feh, at least you were able to find me something new." He tapped his arm, where dozens of symbols were etched into his scales. "I'm running out of space and need to start on the next one."

"We should have simply chosen war," another Sauren, Kolp, stated. "I haven't been on a large hunt in many cycles and haven't seen war since the last tribal war."

"Which caused us to go from forty-three tribes to twenty-nine," Tiox pointed out acerbically. "And the one before that was eighty-six to forty-three—literally half the tribes destroyed or absorbed."

"Maybe that's how it should be. One united Saura under the leadership of the best," Kolp retorted.

"We are hunters, the fiercest warriors, but we are more than that," Seeb stated. "Without the craftsmanship of the Xola tribe, we would not have the weapons we all train and hunt with. Without the Bel'Reve's artists, we would not have the symbols you wear so proudly on your scales."

"And without the Tul'Zera, you wouldn't have the ability to make this hunt." Raza finally spoke up and gestured around the ship. "You can thank us for that too, along with sparing your tribe in that last war, Kolp."

Kolp dragged his claws along his chair and glared at the younger Sauren. "Keep talking like that, and you won't live to see Ken-Wai, youngling!"

Tiox closed his eyes and huffed. "This is why I hate going to the tribal communes."

"We're almost to the arena," the pilot informed them. "I'll bring the ship down and open the viewer so you can take a look."

The sides of the ship retracted and the Sauren looked out to see a golden dome floating above the watery planet. "Elegant, but it'd look better colored in their blood." Jok'sa chuckled.

"Why did we allow them to choose the arena?" Seeb asked Tiox with a frown. "This could give them a clear advantage."

"We chose the combat and they chose the location," the

war chief reminded them. "If you're worried about fighting underwater, maybe you should have prepared better."

"They can choose to fight in space itself," Kolp grunted. "We will still be victorious."

The ship drew up to a dock on the side of the arena and the eleven Sauren walked out. Dozens of Tsuna awaited them. Raza looked around warily. Even though he didn't want to question the elders or sound like he was siding with miscreants like Kolp and Jok'sa, he was worried that this was a trap. Eleven Sauren on a world full of people they were there to essentially conquer didn't make for encouraging odds.

If it came down to an ambush, they would annihilate many of their adversaries, but they wouldn't be able to boast about it. Hopefully, the Tsuna weren't foolish enough to risk all-out war with an unknown race, especially after everything they had done to try to end this with as few casualties as possible.

One approached, holding a box, and Raza and a few others prepared themselves for trouble as he opened it. Inside were eleven small devices. He pointed to one and then to his head. None of the Sauren moved, with the exception of Tiox, who took one of the devices and placed it on his brow.

"Translators," he stated. "They speak with some sort of noise—sound waves or the like that we can't hear naturally. We have to use these, or we can't understand them."

The others looked at one another before they each took one. Once they had put them on, they waited for the Tsuna to talk.

"Checking...can you understand me?" the one with the box asked.

"We can." Tiox nodded. "Are you prepared?"

The emissary shut the box and bowed as another Tsuna, this one in armor with a domed helmet and holding a spear, walked forward. "I assume you are one of the war chiefs of the Sauren?"

"I am Tiox Vorlen of the Hassar tribe," the war chief responded. "How do I address you?"

"Prey," Jok'sa murmured.

The Tsuna removed his helmet to reveal alabaster skin and a bald head. "I will be known as leader. Even with our translators, our names are not so easily understandable, so we shall simply use titles for now." He motioned to ten of his compatriots behind him. "I and my warriors will face you in individual combat, as per the rules of your Rekka, to decide the fate of our world and people."

Tiox studied the Tsuna warriors briefly. "Then I ask again, are you prepared?"

"Are you?" he asked in turn, "This arena has been used by my people for generations. All the warriors here, including myself, have fought within many times. We wished to offer you one day to get to know it so that there can be no recourse or claims of unfair advantage once it ends."

"Generous and foolish—a perfect pair." Kolp chuckled and grimaced as he had forgotten the translator and saw the leader eye him with open disapproval.

"Fine, we will accept those terms and prepare," Tiox confirmed. "Come the next night, we shall begin Rekka."

Although there were cheers from the Sauren, Raza noticed that there wasn't much enthusiasm from the war chief and that Seeb was oddly silent. They entered the arena and when Raza looked back, he saw the Tsuna leader speaking to the war chief.

CHAPTER THREE

Raza watched as two Tsuna warriors practiced, one wielding a rifle and the other a blade. The latter weapon was mostly featureless, a silver color, and it looked more like a paddle than a true blade. But he wielded it expertly, dodged the other warrior's shots, and even deflected them with the flat side of the sword.

"They are quite good, aren't they?" Raza turned as Tiox and Seeb approached. "I have seen them in combat while I and the other war chiefs came here for talks. They fight differently than we do. It's more about form than strength and cunning, but they aren't without power."

Raza took another look as the warrior with the sword disarmed the one with the rifle. "Practicing for gunplay won't do them much good. We hardly use them."

"Jok'sa uses a hand cannon, and Ozil is fond of blasters," Seeb reminded him. "But I think it was a practice of speed and dexterity, not simply dealing with guns."

"They won't be able to deal with us using raw strength so will have to rely on their other advantages in this situa-

JOSHUA ANDERLE & MICHAEL ANDERLE

tion. They are aware of their shortcomings and are looking for the best way to approach. This should be a good fight," Tiox reasoned.

"You sound like you admire them." Raza looked the war chief in the eyes. "Not like one admires a powerful prey, but as a fellow hunter."

The older Sauren was silent for a moment. "I didn't want it to come to this. For all the cycles that we have traveled out into the stars, searching for prey, we have only found beasts, monsters, and ruins. Those are proper hunting grounds, and there is honor in those hunts." The war chief moved his hand across some scars on his chest. "I have seen wars—the tribal wars we spoke of on the vessel. I fought in the last one and saw many of my tribe felled by those they used to call brother. It started over territory—new territory, the planets we were hunting on—then old wounds opened, tempers flared, and we were stuck in a war that continued through three cycles and almost halved the population."

"These are not Sauren," Raza pointed out. "We were not egregious with our demands. Our only request is that they allow us the use of their planet for hunts, for which we pay tribute for the culling of their beasts."

"That was the sticking point. They try not to cull their beasts but train them and allow them to live on their own. They hold their planet's environment sacred," Tiox explained. "I was told that they place the blame of any rampant beast on the actions of the races called the Angula in the deep recesses of their planet. This is a foe they have fought for generations. They see us as another version of that."

"Then these Angula are nothing more than hunters?" Raza questioned. "It seems we would have more in common with them than with these weak people."

"The Angula are not like us. They hunt for the thrill of killing alone, beast or person. Also, they take no trophy and use the beast not for sustenance or progress, but as toys." Tiox grimaced. "I would have no issue hunting them, but these Tsuna show more grace and wisdom, something we need in the Sauren."

Raza looked at Seeb. "You say nothing to this? Do you agree with the war chief?"

Seeb shrugged. "In some respects. I have not spent the time with these Tsuna as he has, but from what he has told me, we could learn from them or at least find some agreement."

"If that is the case, why are you fighting? Why was Rekka chosen to begin with?"

Tiox frowned. "I am the oldest among the war chiefs, old enough to remember that last war. The others...well, some are wise and know the potential boons of meeting another race, learning their ways, and making pacts. But most of the others...imagine if Jok'sa and Kolp were war chiefs."

"I can't imagine we would get much accomplished," Raza grumbled. "But why are you fighting, specifically, if you feel so strongly about this?"

Tiox clenched his jaw and looked at Seeb for a moment. "I will not fight them. None of us will."

"What are you talking about?" Raza demanded. "Why are we here, then? Rekka has already been declared. It cannot be undone."

"When a war chief dies, what happens, Ran'ama?" Seeb asked.

"The passing ceremony, What of it?"

"Before that—the dying words."

"When a dying war chief makes a request, if the one who follows upholds it, that will become rule." Raza's eyes widened and he gripped Tiox by his arm. "What are you planning?"

The war chief looked at him, his expression grim. "Even should we win Rekka, there is no guarantee that this will make the Tsuna obey us for all time. There would also be this Angula threat to deal with." He wrenched his arm from the younger Sauren's grasp. "We are not what we once were. Our advancements have made us believe that we deserve to be known as the greatest among the stars. But we are but a hundred million and lose proud hunters every day. We should keep our traditions up without succumbing to the instincts of our prey."

He sighed and fixed his gaze on the Tsuna. "Kolp said we should all be united under one tribe, the strongest, and it reminded me of one of our legends that said we should do the opposite—about how the tribes started in the first place." He breathed in deeply and closed his eyes.

"Many, many cycles ago, when the tribes weren't yet born, the Sauren roamed only across the land. We were all hunters, the apex of Saura, but that was all we saw ourselves as. One day, a monstrous Sauren, said to stand as tall as the trees, declared himself the alpha. Anyone who fought against his will was slain by his claws. He ruled for many cycles like this, demanded tribute, and feasted on the weaker Sauren. Then, several other Sauren, great warriors themselves, came together. They were not only warriors, though, and all practiced different disciplines. Their thought was that if they came together—each unique in their own right—they could accomplish what most saw as the new rule."

Raza nodded. "I've heard this old tale. They slew this alpha Sauren, and others became their disciples—the first tribes. The Tul'Zera are among them, supposedly begun by two of those warriors, a female tactician and a male champion."

The war chief nodded. "Many grew from then on, each with their own culture and practices. At least until the wars, where those cherished differences became something to mock or dismiss." Tiox sighed. "I see these Tsuna as a tribe of their own. They call them clans, but they live by similar paths. I would rather die than see another tribal war take place." He clicked his claws together, his face resolute. "So I will. I will let their leader claim me and request that there will be no war among us when I pass my title to Seeb."

The younger Sauren's jaw was so rigid, it felt like he would snap his teeth. "This plan is madness. Do you think that will stop a potential war? Especially if you let their leader kill you. Where is your honor?"

"Lost when I killed dozens of my brethren," Tiox snapped in response. "Seeb will make sure my will is done. The other war chiefs will agree. If they hold their titles dear, they will uphold the traditions."

"He is not even of your tribe," Raza challenged.

"The war chiefs watch over all the Sauren. They were established after the wars so that there would be those who had the interest of the race at heart. We are the chiefs who rose from war." Tiox pressed a claw against Raza's chest to make his point. "Our tribes may be our family, but we need to remember that what we are—all of us—is fueled by the best of us. Seeb may not be of my tribe, but I know that he will watch over you and make sure this comes to pass."

"You would die for those things?" Raza asked and gestured impatiently at the warriors below. "For a race of beings we didn't even know existed half a cycle ago? If I knew I would be responsible for the death of a war chief, I would never have reported this finding."

"Is that so?" Tiox questioned harshly. "That wouldn't have been very honorable of you."

Raza snapped his teeth and looked away. "Have you told the others as well?"

"Almost everyone else I handpicked explicitly for this reason." The war chief placed his hands upon the railing. "I haven't told Jok'sa or Kolp. I doubt they would agree or that they would allow it to happen. Honestly, I didn't want them to come, but their tribal leaders and another war chief requested them, and I had to make sure that nothing was suspicious. It will be too late for them to do anything come tomorrow."

"And the Tsuna leader? He agreed to this?" Raza growled his frustration. "To take the life of one so selfishly when he has been given the chance to fight for his people?"

"It's not so one-sided, Ran'ama," Seeb explained in an effort to calm him. "The leader agreed to the plan but offered himself in exchange. He will go to Saura to face the war chiefs' judgment."

"If this was done at Tiox's behest, he will face no recourse. What good is that?"

In an unexpected motion, the older Sauren snatched Raza's throat and caught both him and Seeb by surprise. Tiox hauled him in close and looked him squarely in the eye. "As I said, to keep our people from falling even lower. We are hunters, not conquerors."

Raza grabbed his leader's arm and managed to push himself free from the vice-like grasp. "Why tell me any of this?" he demanded and felt his throat for injury. "Because I was another you were simply forced to bring? Did you want to see if I would be a problem in your plan?"

"There was that possibility." Tiox nodded. "But I also knew you would take it the hardest. As you said, you were one of those who discovered this planet. You would feel responsible for the events that happened, even if they were above your rank and far out of your control."

Raza fell silent and exhaled a long, ragged breath. "When will this happen?"

"Tomorrow. At the start of the ceremony, I will declare my intention and it will commence." Tiox spoke calmly and with great resolution.

Raza looked at the warriors again, who had begun to depart. "Do you truly think this is worth it?"

"You may not be a youngling, but you are still young, Ran'ama," the war chief replied. "I am but one life, and this will save millions and leave the Sauren to grow. We didn't even know that the Tsuna existed, but what of other life? Should we fight them all?"

"We should—" Raza turned and studied the weary face of the old hunter, the sorrowful but resolute visage, and caught a glimpse of the memories in his mind. He hadn't been there to experience them, but he could almost read them upon his leader's face. "We are Sauren and we prove ourselves in combat. Even the creationists of the Tul'Zera believe they are battling in the field of the mind."

"Combat is made up of battle, passion, honor, and sacrifice," Seeb pointed out.

"And I am sacrificing for our future," Tiox finished. "You will see that one day, but I have only one request of you."

"What is it you require, War Chief?" Raza asked and bowed to the elder.

"Learn from this that our place as Sauren is something that is to be proved time and again so that no one will ever question it." Tiox bared his fangs in a grin. "If nothing else, it will make our potential allies hold us in high regard and maybe make a statue in our honor one day."

Raza, despite his brooding, laughed. "I will certainly make sure it gets done. This, I can promise."

The event arrived. Raza watched from the stands with trepidation as Tiox walked forward into the center of the ring. He kept his gaze focused on the Tsuna to make sure that nothing and no one would stop this.

"Tsuna!" Tiox called out in ringing tones. "I, as war chief of my people, will declare that this Rekka is no more. It will not proceed." This caused surprised gasps and confused murmurs in the crowd.

"I believe that your people and my people have much to

learn. We are both surprised by new intelligent races amongst the stars and beginning this new relationship with needless slaughter is unnecessary." He drew a deep breath and focused on the Tsuna warrior leader. "My people are mired in old ways. Traditions are held dear by us, but as they should be respected, so must the change of time be too. We are proud hunters and have lived life by codes and honor, and I shall make sure that nothing befalls your people. With my dying words, I shall say that the Sauren will not hunt on your planet and ask that you be open to my people after these wounds have healed."

The Tsuna leader stepped forward. "I have discussed much with this Sauren war chief. I did not wish to keep you in the dark." He looked back at his warriors and bowed his head. "But this was a delicate situation and this plan pains me." He drew a blade. Raza noted immediately that it was of Sauren design and even their scales couldn't withstand it. "This champion will give his life to assure our peace. Remember him for this. I will also lay my life down in the name of peace and offer myself to the Sauren after this task."

This caused some frantic yells and shouts from both races. Raza was unmoved, but he wouldn't look away. He would learn this lesson, one of giving yourself up for something greater, of knowing when to follow traditions and when to rebuke them for worthy goals.

The leader looked at the war chief, who nodded. "I declare Seeb Boka A'zul of the Tul'Zera tribe as my successor."

"You will do no such thing," a voiced roared and was followed by a loud blast. The Tsuna leader toppled with a hole in his chest. Raza rushed down from the balcony as the Tsuna cried out in shock. Jok'sa walked onto the field with his hand cannon pointed at the war chief as the Tsuna warriors ran over, some to the body of the leader and others around Tiox.

"Jok'sa? I left Ozil and Es'pic to guard you," the war chief shouted as he moved to draw his razor disk.

"And you will join them now," Jok'sa yelled in response and fired a single shot into the war chiefs' heart. Raza stopped in shock. Tsuna raced past him as Tiox's blood sprayed in a pulsing arc before he collapsed. "By right of Rekka, by having felled a war chief, I will be named his successor."

Seeb attacked from above. He barreled into the killer and clawed at his arms to knock his gun away. "You scum. What have you done?"

"I wouldn't let a coward control me," he bellowed furiously and dug a claw into his assailant's eye. Seeb reared back in pain and the assassin followed through with a headbutt to drive him off before he snatched up his hand cannon. "Like you have." He fired and Seeb whipped his tail at the shot, exploded it, and hurled them both away, his tail and most of his back split by the blast.

Raza flung himself from the stands and onto the traitor. Jok'sa tried to fire at him but he forced his arm up so the blast rocketed into the roof and shattered the ceiling. The Tsuna warriors fled. As the younger Sauren bit down on his adversary's neck and sunk his claws into his chest, Jok'sa roared in pain. The ceiling fell, and he dug in deeper before he spun and careened the other Sauren into the falling debris. He landed hard and before he could recover, a large section of the ceiling collapsed on top of him.

The still somewhat dazed young warrior hastened to the corpse of the Tsuna leader, retrieved his blade, and approached the debris. Jok'sa struggled to free himself and Raza held the blade aloft. The assassin hissed and cursed him, telling him he was as much a coward as the others had been. Without a word, he arced the blade down into his skull. Jok'sa's eyes went white. Raza yanked the blade out and with one mighty swing, sliced the traitor's head off.

He spiked the blade into the decapitated head and ran over to Seeb. "Are you all right?"

"The war chief?" Seeb asked and winced from the pain. "Is he—"

Raza glanced at their leader and shook his head. The shot was through the heart and there was no visible regeneration. "He's gone, I'm sorry. If there is nothing else, he accomplished what he wanted to do. You are now war chief and must bring his plans to fruition."

Seeb grimaced as the young warrior helped him up. The Tsuna circled around them and Raza eyed them warily. Would they strike? Their leader had said he would give his life, and even without that, they couldn't think this was a ruse when their war chief was dead and they had killed Jok'sa.

One of them moved forward, his weapon at the ready. "Will your plan succeed?"

Raza looked at Seeb in surprise. "Our new war chief lives. Once he is recovered, he will make our last war chief's words law. We vow this."

The warrior looked at the others. "Where are the other Sauren? Are they also traitors?"

"Ozil and Es'pic may be dead, from what Jok'sa said," Seeb muttered and managed to stand without support. "But the others should be here soon after all the ruckus."

"Seeb!" They turned at a shout and a group of Sauren raced toward them. The Tsuna warriors readied for an attack, but the one in front had them stand down. Raza nodded in thanks. As Seeb explained to them what had happened, Raza noted a wrathful glare in Kolp's eye. The older Sauren walked to Tiox's body and yanked the blade from Jok'sa's head on the way. He placed it on the former war chief's chest, then crossed his arms over it. He would make sure he had a hunter's funeral and one day, he would be sure that sacrifice was taught to be as important as honor and battle.

CHAPTER FOUR

R aza withdrew to his quarters after talking with the delegates. The trip to the embassy wouldn't take too long once they reached the warp gate, but he already felt restless. On hunts, he could occupy himself with tactics and checking his gear, but during these delegation missions, he couldn't even plan. Half the time, he didn't know what they wanted, and the other half was usually wasted by someone asking for a report.

They were paranoid, those humans. In the cycles since the Rekka, the Sauren and Tsuna had moved from an uneasy truce to allies. The Sauren received a lot of work from their scientists to explore the universe and bring back samples, and many stayed to help them against the Angula threat.

In that time, Raza made the rank of Ken-ra and was a leader of his own pack. Their first mission was to find a rare creature, a borroth, a vicious titan with an outer shell that was almost indestructible and a ram on its head that could crush even a Sauren.

When they arrived, they saw their quarry carried away by a ship. They contacted other tribes to see who else was on-world, but no one claimed responsibility. When they contacted the Tsuna, they explained that they had no scientists or warriors in that sector but asked them to describe the ship. After the explanation, they were informed that they had seen a human vessel.

That was first contact with them, even if it was merely a fleeting glance and one-sided. Raza wondered if it was a sense of fate that led him to be one of the first to see two new races. Whatever it might be, he was glad he didn't have to be the first one to see the Mirus, the only race that generally concerned him. He found it both amusing and upsetting that the humans seemed to trust them more than the Sauren.

He thought back to their first battle. While waiting to assume his responsibilities as a newly appointed war chief, he'd elected to make one final run with his pack, who were instructed to pursue the humans and retrieve the quarry. At first, they went in simply for recon, but they had discovered that they held the borroth at a station, not their planet. The location was well armed, but they were able to sneak aboard and discover where the creature was secured.

One of the defense droid devices discovered them, and a battle ensued. They fought for at least two days, during which Raza attempted to make it a priority to simply retrieve the borroth and leave. The humans attacked first, but their fear was understandable. At that time, they had just met the Tsuna and now, they confronted the Sauren. He recalled when he first met the aliens. They had been shocked to realize how vast the universe was. To meet another race on board a private vessel trying to steal something of theirs without introduction was probably more than they could handle.

Raza hadn't thought that way at the time. He held no interest in the humans in the beginning. They seemed a soft race, like the Tsuna. Their technology was refined but seemed needlessly complex. Perhaps if he had taken Tiox's words to heart he would have tried diplomacy first, but his hunter's blood boiled too hot, and he couldn't show weakness as a new pack leader. Unlike the Tsuna, there was no bargaining and no attempt at diplomacy at first, merely battle. But he would have his opportunity after a time. They battled for five earth days. For three of them, he was alone in a fight against the first human he would eventually call a friend.

"Are the sharpshooters ready?" an ensign asked.

"Most of them were wiped out in sector D," a recruit responded. "The ones that are still kicking are in position, but there aren't great spots. We'll have to lead these monsters into the clear area."

"You make it sound so easy," another recruit muttered as he took out his empty magazine and reloaded. "Did they get through the doors yet?"

"Two of them, and they're about to take down a third," a security guard said. "After that, the one in front of us is the only one between us and them."

"How many of us are left?" the ensign questioned and looked around.

"There are forty-eight of us here, between navy, marines, and security. Back-up is on the way, sir," a petty officer responded.

"Who's the backup?" Before anyone could answer, the doors literally erupted. Six armored Sauren stood in the entrance and growled as they held their weapons at the ready.

"They're here," a recruit shouted unnecessarily.

"Fire! Get them into the clear area," the ensign ordered as he brought his machine gun up and fired.

Raza roared at the defenders and the mask of his helmet did little to muffle the bloodthirsty cry. He pointed a claw to direct his pack at the troop, and all roared as they attacked the humans. The lasers of the men's guns did little to his shields and their kinetic rounds dented his armor but did nothing to his skin. He drew his hunter's lance and crouched.

"The leader," one of the recruits warned before his head erupted from a blaster shot.

"Here he comes," another yelled. The guards and military men backed away as the assault continued but they fanned out so the Sauren couldn't sweep them all together. Ken'ra took an explosive bola from his belt. He cast it toward one of the soldiers in heavy armor and it whipped around his chest and ensnared him. When the ends connected, it erupted, knocked some of the other soldiers down, and blew the soldier to bits.

Lok aimed and fired a round from his gauntlet to strike another soldier in the chest. When the bolt impacted, it injected something into the armor, which started to melt

"What the hell is this?" the soldier yelled and quickly whipped the armor off and examined his chest.

"Some sort of acid. We don't know what the enemies are carrying, so be careful," the ensign shouted. "When will that backup get here?"

"They said eta is five minutes," another recruit shouted as he backstepped and continued to fire. He managed to hit a Sauren in the leg with a charged shot. He celebrated as it roared, but it was cut short when the alien turned and lurched at him. He yelled as he tried to fire, but his attacker knocked the gun away.

"You keep it distracted and I'll get him," the ensign ordered and raced to assist the endangered recruit

"On it," the petty officer hollered. He turned and fired at the Sauren, who glowered at him and snarled. A guard raced up with a Tesla cannon and fired a charged shot. It shocked the alien, and its limbs and tail flailed. The ensign grasped the recruit with one arm and dropped a grenade at the alien's feet as they scrambled out of reach. It detonated to blow the Sauren's armor off with enough force to launch it to the ceiling where it thudded solidly before it dropped. The momentary anticipation of joy at finally claiming a casualty was quashed when the creature simply glared at them and hissed its outrage, now even angrier than before.

"Can we even kill these things?" one asked.

"I've seen them bleed," the ensign said as he lowered the recruit he'd rescued and vented his weapon. "That means we can kill them. Sharpshooters, fire!"

A dozen shots powered into the unarmored Sauren from the floor above, and he roared in distress before he sank to the floor with a hiss. Raza flipped a switch on his lance and launched it upward. It soared over a group of three of the snipers, missed them, and exploded against the wall to kill them all.

Lok selected another sniper and fired one of his acid bolts at the man's helmet. The acid poured in and scalded his face and the hapless soldier struggled to remove his helmet before he simply slumped and went still. The battle continued and the Sauren made the snipers their priority, with the exception of Raza. He looked at the ensign, who appeared to be this group's leader, and charged him. The man fired first, then retrieved another grenade and threw it. Raza smacked it with the back of his hand and launched it up to the floor above where it exploded and killed a sniper hiding there.

He careened toward the ensign and his claws cut through the machine gun, but as he went in for the kill, he was distracted by a bright purple light beside him. Raza raised an arm and activated a shield a split second before a metal fist caught him in the face.

The force was massive and hurled Raza, the ensign, and anyone else around it back a few paces. The Sauren impacted with a wall and cracked it with his armor, but he rolled onto his feet almost instantly, his razor disk at the ready. In front of him was a large man with close-cropped blond hair and a goatee. He held a metal gauntlet up with a cylinder on top and said something in their language but glared at him as he spoke. The man looked at him quizzically before he smacked his own head with the other hand and retrieved a Tsuna translator device.

"Do you understand me now, you scaly git?" he asked.

The Sauren understood, but some of the words were still odd. What was a git?

"How did you like this force gauntlet?" the man asked and flexed his hand. "It's something they've been working on. They used scales from that rhino-looking thing we have on Voinik to make the plating. It's one of the few things that could stand up to the force."

The arm of Raza's suit was shattered and the gauntlet with the barrier shield lay smashed on the floor. He lowered his arm and growled as he glared at the man as his pack approached.

"It looks like I pissed you off pretty good." The human chuckled, seemingly not worried about approaching death. "I've heard of you from the files—Sauren, right? I thought you and the Tsuna were chummy."

"We have a pact with the Tsuna but none with you," Raza snapped.

"Really? How do we get one?" he inquired. "That would be better than all this pointless bloodshed, right?"

"What are you doing?" the ensign yelled. "Shut the hell up and take them down." He looked around, clearly alarmed. "Where are your men? I was told I would have backup."

"They are evacuating the civilians. Don't worry yourself about them. I'm here, aren't I?" he said dismissively, his attention on Raza. "Forget the whiner. You have me."

"Do you think you can handle me and my pack?" Raza snarled. "We have killed many of you as we have ascended this station in search of our prey."

"Your prey? That's not us? Are you looking for some-thing in particular?"

"The borroth—the beast you took from Voinik. We were charged with its capture and you are blocking our way."

"So you want the beastie." The man nodded and stroked his goatee. "I'm starting to put it together. Fine, if that's what you want, I'll prep it and you can have it."

"Sergeant!" the ensign cried indignantly. "That is not in your authority to—"

"Quiet, boyo. I'm dealing with this."

"We do not make deals," another Sauren, Ketik, stated coldly. "You have impeded our progress and took something that wasn't yours."

"To be fair, you broke into our station," the human pointed out. "This one is close to Earth too. This could turn into a declaration of war."

"Let them...come..." The downed Sauren muttered as he planted one hand on the floor and forced himself up. "You are...not...a challenge."

"We filled him full of holes," a recruit shouted, and the ensign gaped in incredulous horror.

"They regenerate. You should have gone for the heart or brain," the sergeant explained. He glanced at the ensign and shrugged. "Or blown it up. That probably would have worked."

"I did. It only destroyed the armor," the ensign shot back.

"You should have shoved it down its gullet. Seriously, you should read more docs."

As the soldier glowered, Raza spoke again. "While my Jah-Wai speaks out of turn, we will not accept your deal."

"Oh no? Why's that?"

"You have claimed the beast so we must fight for the right of the hunt," the leader explained. "If you had run off, that would suffice, but you continue to fight. We must therefore respond in kind."

"Odd and somewhat noble, but mostly idiotic." He sighed. "I tell you what, how about a round of Rekka or whatever."

Raza blinked and studied the human cautiously. "You know our rituals?"

"Only that one. I recently got a doc on you guys from the Tsuna before you launched your assault. They wanted to introduce us to each other, but I think we're fairly well acquainted now."

"You know what the combat entails, right?" Raza asked.

"It's a fight to the death. I'm good on the specifics." He folded his arms and puffed his chest out. "You look like the leader, so you and me will go. If you win, you claim the beastie and whatever you like. If I win, get the hell off this station and we'll call you when we feel like being chummy."

"You realize that by 'claim anything' you mean he could claim anyone on this station, sergeant?" the ensign protested.

"Then I would say you'd best do your damndest not to be here," he answered without breaking his focus on the Sauren. "And take those still alive with you. I'll hold them off."

The ensign stood and shook his head. "They've killed over thirty men and we hardly put a scratch on them. This is a fool's errand."

"Maybe, but I'm a hell of a tough fool. Now, what do you say, lizard man?"

Raza looked at his pack and nodded. "I cannot refuse an outright contest if it's one on one. If your warriors withdraw, mine will as well."

"You got it." He finally looked at the ensign. "Get going. I'll hold 'em off for as long as you need."

The other man's anger faded. "Good luck," he said quietly, looked at a soldier with a shotgun, and motioned for him to toss it. He caught it and handed it to Wolfson.

"I have my own," he said and gestured at the rifle on his back. "But options are nice, thanks."

The ensign nodded and saluted smartly. "Everyone, retreat to escape pods and transports," he ordered and the remaining soldiers raced off to the other side of the sector. Raza motioned for his pack to leave.

Ketik helped their last comrade off the floor and Ken'ra said, "We shall await your return. I expect you won't be too long."

Raza tilted his head to observe the man thoughtfully. "This one seems different, but I'm sure that I will be successful."

"Good hunting." Ken'ra nodded and left the sector to head back to their ship.

Raza and the man stood, unmoving. "It is customary to announce yourself before we fight," he declared and held his claws up. "I am Ran'ama Aboren Zin'til Arcquini, a War Chief of the Sauren."

"That's a mouthful, Ran'ama Abor. I caught the first letters, but how about simply Raza?"

"You would not even let me have my name?" he asked and growled with real affront.

"No offense meant, but it's a mouthful." The man held

his gloved hand up. "I guess I should tell you the name of the man who is about to kick your ass, huh? I'm Staff Sergeant Baioh Wolfson of the United Earth Army."

"And you are my prey," Raza stated coldly as he lowered to the floor with his claws at the ready.

"And you'll be my new pair of boots," Wolfson retorted as he pressed a switch on the gauntlet to power it up again.

Raza roared and launched forward. He tried to thrust them both into a slide, but the human simply slammed his fist into the floor. Instead of another explosion of force, a massive wave of electricity surged and the Sauren jerked for a few seconds before he jumped back, his tail still twitching.

"Did you like that?" Wolfson yelled as he ran up to his opponent and activated the switch again. Raza noted that it switched from white to purple. "I have a couple of different settings on this beauty. Is this what you were looking for?" Raza dodged a few jabs before the man raised his hand up to swing it down on his head. He caught the gauntlet and bared his teeth at his attacker.

The sergeant grinned, pressed the switch, and held it down. The light grew bright before it faded out as another explosion erupted, but this one wasn't nearly as strong. It was enough to make the alien stumble but not enough to compel him to release the gauntlet, even though Wolfson tried to pry it out of his grasp. He snarled as he ripped the gauntlet off the man's hand and tried to crush it, but it wouldn't give. Remembering that his adversary had said it was made from the borroth's hide, he drove it into the soldier's stomach. Wolfson gasped and doubled over. The Sauren pounded it over his head before he raised one of his massive clawed legs and kicked his chest to force him to his knees.

"Are you gonna slap me this whole fight?" Wolfson grunted as he stood and retrieved the shotgun. "Show me those claws."

Raza took the bait and swiped at the soldier. The heavy armor was enough to block each strike momentarily and he shoved the shotgun into the alien's throat and fired. The blast staggered the creature and he coughed from the force of it. Wolfson ran up and swung the butt of the gun into his stomach before he fired into his jaw. Raza roared when his helmet shattered. He thrust the shotgun aside as the man tried to fire again, clawed at his face, and raked across his cheek.

The sergeant ducked but caught a kick from the Sauren. He drew his rifle with his other hand, spun around to avoid another slash from the vicious claws, and slammed the butt of the weapon into his opponent's head before he fired both guns. Raza was forced back when his shields and armor cracked apart. He grasped his razor disk and flung it, but Wolfson dodged it easily before the alien called it back and it sliced through his rifle on its return arc.

"Shit!" Wolfson cried. He jumped to the side as Raza advanced slowly and controlled the disk as he did so. The soldier tried to dodge the attacks, but it cut through his chest and left thigh. He holstered his shotgun and dove to the floor. The Sauren flipped the disk in the air and it altered course toward him. He twisted and caught it in the gauntlet he'd recovered and grinned at his adversary.

Raza smiled in return, pressed a switch on his gauntlet, and the disk blinked alarmingly. Wolfson hurled it away quickly, but it exploded, and shards ripped into his back and side. He cried out and toppled and the alien took the opportunity to activate his wrist-blade and advance.

The man scrambled to his feet and raced toward his opponent. He fired his shotgun as he drew closer and the Sauren raised an arm and fired a net charge from his gauntlet. Wolfson flung himself aside and rolled. He found his feet as Raza raced into the attack and he fired two more shots before his gun overheated. There was barely time to vent the weapon before the alien was on him and slashed at him with his claws and blade in a rage. Wolfson ducked and strafed to the side, dropped his shotgun, and drew a kinetic pistol. The Sauren yanked a whip from his belt and as the man turned to fire, he snapped the pistol out of his hand. He cracked the whip and struck at his adversary, who rolled and retrieved his shotgun before he barreled into the alien and slammed the open vent into his exposed chest. The heat of the core burned and the creature roared and snapped at his attacker, who withdrew.

Raza brought the whip back and snapped it forward again. Wolfson weaved around the strikes until he was able to catch it in his gauntlet. He pulled and tried to haul the alien to him, but the creature pulled back and was certainly stronger than he was. The man dropped his gun and fumbled behind him. He winced as he eased a piece of the razor disk from his back and used it to cut the whip.

"Do you still wanna play with your toys?" Wolfson asked snidely. Raza growled and straightened to his full height to reveal his claws and massive body. "Good, now we can get into the thick of it."

Their battle continued for days. After their initial fight, they stalked each other through the mostly empty station. Raza developed a fondness for the soldier during their extended skirmishes. When the Sauren were officially invited to the new embassy as one of the known races, Wolfson was there to greet him. The crazy soldier had even learned his name.

That had, in its own weird way, somehow clinched their friendship, even if he'd let him call him Raza from then on.

There was a knock on his door. "It's open."

A hunter walked in, dressed in full gear, and bowed. "War Chief, we are approaching the embassy."

Raza's eyes widened as he looked out the window. He hadn't even realized they had gone through the warp gate "How long?"

"Four hours at most at our current speed."

Raza huffed his irritation. "Prepare my personal ship."

"Sir?"

"I want to meet someone. In my ship, I can do that and be at the embassy before you finish docking.

The hunter nodded. "It'll be done chief."

CHAPTER FIVE

As Raza flew toward Earth, a comm link notification popped onto his screen. The code was Wolfson's, but the ID number wasn't. "Who is this?" he answered.

A screen appeared to display a man with jet-black hair and a pale complexion. He wore a helmet with the Nexus Academy Symbol on it. "War Chief Ran'ama, this is Security Officer Jetton. I have an urgent request from Head Officer Wolfson. He hoped you would be available."

"Speak, Officer."

"Wolfson is in pursuit of a fugitive known as Gin Sonny. He's downed all our ships, but the HO is in pursuit. He sent me his tracking signal and asked you to join him in apprehending him."

"Gin Sonny? The revenant?" Wolfson had told him about his encounter with Kaiden. Raza was already familiar with the wretch. He was responsible for the death of an entire pack during his first days as War Chief.

Raza felt a chill as he watched the screen. This was where they were felled. He had sent a hunter to look into the distress call of a human science group on an outpost in Kal'ah as the Sauren had been close. The screen he watched was a feed from the hunter's ocular camera. He watched the events unfold.

The view was dark and most of the lights were out. The hunter curled his hand and his wrist blades emerged when he saw blood along the floor. He walked toward the rear window in the room. No light from star or moon came through it. His movement cautious, he peered out and saw nothing. There were no trees or animals on this planet and the scientists had been there to study microorganisms. There was merely a dark horizon that seemed to stretch endlessly.

The last of the lights went out and the hunter held his blades at the ready as he attempted to find the cause of these killings. He walked through the halls and checked each room as he progressed. So far, he'd found nothing. He wondered if the person who had committed this massacre was somewhere within or if they had already fled. The blood was fresh, and he had arrived almost as soon as the request was sent. Still, he was too late.

A crash resounded some distance ahead. The hunter raced to the lab and kicked the door in. No one was there.

He crossed to the far side of the room and saw that a few empty tubes had fallen. They had perhaps rolled off the table, or they were knocked down by the killer.

Satisfied that there was no one there, he left the room and continued to the last place he needed to check—the observation room. He opened the double doors and looked around the barren room. Three walls were made of glass and a lone table stood in the middle. Everything else seemed to be boxed up or pushed against the walls. Obviously, they hadn't even finished setting up. He saw no one and nothing seemed disturbed. Had he missed something? Had the killer already left?

He froze and squinted into the shadowed space. Some of the dust on the floor had drifted up slightly as if someone or something moved along the floor. He felt an unnerving chill along his spine, the same unease as when he first faced an Anjan during his trial. He followed his instincts, threw himself to the ground, and rolled. A split second later, he heard wood splinter behind him. He stood and gaped at the wall that had been newly savaged. Two long gashes slashed into it and the floor at the base was scarred by the same assault. Someone or something was definitely there, and he could not see it.

His instincts overwhelmed him, and he leapt to the side, but something collided with him and he tumbled at the impact. Quickly, he scrambled to his feet and moved back. An intense pain below his ribs drew a gasped protest and he looked down at a deep incision through his armor and skin. Blood flowed down his stomach and thigh as he steadied himself. He retrieved an orb and threw it down and his visor darkened despite the already inky environment. The orb erupted into a bright light. The hunter could see something cloaked—a figure shimmered amongst the illumination but remained almost intangible.

The light seemed to contort around the being's body, but no features were present. It appeared to the hunter to be humanoid. He marked along the floor to create an ember trail with a plasma blade.

The being attacked in a frenzy. The light from the orb faded as the Sauren prepared to defend himself. He dodged one of its lethal blows and attempted to slice through his adversary, but his blades found no purchase. He lit the room again with another orb, but the creature had disappeared.

He moved forward cautiously and waited for his enemy to attack again while he wondered what or who this was. This killer was unlike the beasts and warriors he had fought before. Its movements were erratic, and the blades cut deep. Even his armor and scales would not be enough. He could deduce that from the marks it had left on him. Yet despite his concerns, a thrill coursed through him. He stopped in the middle of the room when the light from the orb faded again.

He would let this killer come to him.

Despite the logic of that decision, apprehension crept in while he waited for a sound or an attack to pinpoint this creature's location. He would wait for it to strike and grab hold of it. That would, hopefully, provide the opportunity to end it in one blow

A crackling noise emanated from his mask when he chuckled. This would make a good trophy and a good story. He checked his stomach and confirmed that the wound had closed and only dry blood caked his hand. A small twist of the knob on his mask amplified the sound around him. He heard a familiar hum and realized that the plasma blade was closing in—the killer was about to strike. From above and behind the glass panels there, he heard the hum. How had his attacker gotten up there so quickly?

The glass shattered as the killer burst through it from above. The hunter roared and thrust both blades up. They collided with something metallic. It was a distraction. Something pierced his back and he roared in pain and spun to claw the attacker. He found nothing once again and the blade was ripped out of him an instant later. The killer vanished once again.

The hunter continued to hiss in pain but felt it subside after a moment. The unknown assailant had attacked him with a normal blade, thankfully. The plasma could cut right through him, and his regeneration would not be able to heal him quickly enough. Beyond the brief sense of relief, he realized that the killer was toying with him.

He knew that the assailant would not give him another chance to collect himself. His senses already prickled with the certain knowledge that the invisible being was behind him. He spun and even in the almost darkness, the dust on the floor shifted again. Small marks appeared on the floor as the killer dragged its deadly armaments.

The hunter fell back as the creature leapt towards him and dust swirled and danced in the air. He landed a little awkwardly, took his lance out and opened it, and stiffened when something crashed beside him. The killer had obviously fallen to avoid the spike. He rolled away as his attacker finally made a sound—a cough, followed by a chuckle.

He finally saw it. The transparent cloak had fallen, and the killer's white armor appeared, caked with the blood of the scientists. The figure wore a helmet with no features other than a yellow visor, and he twirled the blades in his hands.

The Sauren held his spear at the ready and tightened his grip as the killer once again fell silent and stood completely still. With casual ease, he tossed the plasma blade up into the air and caught it. The hunter needed to take this opportunity to end it, so he thrust forward. However, before his blade could cleave the armored form, the creature spoke.

"This will be my first time killing a Sauren." He chuckled in a masked voice before he disappeared once again.

The tearing of floors and the shattering of glass filled the short silence. He turned to gape as the room was methodically ripped apart by the once-again-invisible horror. With a sigh, he retrieved the last of his illumination orbs and activated it in an attempt to find some sign of his prey. His hunter role changed in an instant

He fell when pain erupted in his left leg and grimaced at a deep wound across his hamstring. Gritting his teeth, he pushed to his feet, propped himself up with his lance, and tried to focus. The killer continued to toy with him and attacked at random, using his lack of vision against him.

The hunter leaned back and hopped out of the lab on his good leg and back into the main building. He used the wall to help him limp down the hall. It seemed certain that his attacker would soon follow. In fact, that was his hope.

The halls were narrow with low ceilings, which gave him a chance to fight. Once the creature pursued him, he only had to concern himself with striking what was in front of him. He wouldn't have to worry about it flanking him. As he turned and positioned himself, his spear at the ready, the outpost fell silent.

The hunter could see the remainder of the observation room through the doorway. It had been torn asunder. Some walls were covered in markings and glowed ember, and all the glass had been broken. However, the killer seemed to have vanished. He began to second-guess himself. His gaze darted around in search of some sign of where he would strike.

He checked his leg. The wound was healing rapidly but he still couldn't put much weight on it. He moved back with small steps and constantly checked his surroundings. Then, as he passed the lab, he realized his mistake. He saw the open window and it dawned on him—when the creature simply attacked at random, he'd thought he was simply trying to mock him and put him on edge. But this was a trick. The killer would attempt to ambush him through another opening.

He had to leave the outpost building. There were too many opportunities for the unseen assailant to strike. He hobbled to the window and threw his spear to the ground before he lifted himself out and jumped unceremoniously to the damp ground below. Ignoring the pain that surged in his leg, he studied his surroundings.

A loud whump made him spin around to look at the roof. He activated the light on his mask and the killer's cloak warped around the bright light thanks to the darkness of the world. The form leapt from the roof and directly toward him.

The hunter had little time to react. He had to decide between dodging the blow or trying to counter. With his leg still mending, he wouldn't be able to move quickly enough to avoid the attack, so he grasped his spear tightly and lunged forward. It struck something but immediately bounced off. The warped cloaking against the light indicated that the killer aimed at his head, so he tilted away and hoped to avoid a direct blow. Blood spewed hotly down his face and the killer laughed, the eerie sound amplified by his mask.

He stumbled back before his opponent landed on top of him. The cloaked assailant once again became visible, but the shimmering light of a shield illuminated him now. The hunter gasped at the stinging pain from his damaged eye and pressed a hand to it to try to numb it. The killer stepped forward and he lunged at the murderous figure in an attempt to stab him with his spear. His adversary simply glided his blade along the haft and cut deep into his claws.

The Sauren hissed and dropped the spear. Before he could react, the killer thrust forward and drove both blades into the hunter. "I've heard that you were supposed to be the best killers around these parts," he mocked.

"We are hunters," the Sauren shouted and pressed a switch on his belt that released an electrical discharge. It forced his assailant back into the darkness and disrupted his shielding. The hunter brought out his wrist blades once more and attacked. "And you are our prey," he roared as he pinned the killer with his light and thrust his blades into him.

They went through—not his chest but his body, which shimmered and faded.

"Are you so sure about that?" Heat streaked across his neck and his breath left him as his neck burned, cut by the plasma blade. The hunter collapsed and clutched the wound as the killer bent and undid his mask. He tilted his head as he studied the fallen Sauren. "Man, you are an ugly motherfucker."

He swung his claws in an attempt at one more strike, but the killer leaned back and grabbed the hand to skewer it on his blade.

"I've heard that you guys have a damn good healing ability. It's not much good against a plasma blade, but still good," he mused before he yanked the blade out and peered through the hole. "I'd like to test it out, but my guess is that more of you are probably coming and as much as it would amuse me to think you're the best they have, I really doubt it."

In a disdainful gesture, he let the hunter's hand drop and leaned over him. "What's that little shine in your eye? Is that a recorder? Am I playing to an audience?" The killer chuckled and placed a hand on his chest. "Well, to anyone watching, I hope you enjoyed my performance, and if you wish to follow my shows, the name is Gin Sonny. Remember that now." He glanced at the struggling hunter. "Man, you can go for a while without breath, huh? I heard that to make sure you're dead, I gotta remove something important." He stowed the plasma blade and held up his curved metal one. "Let's see how well my girl Macha here can get through that skin. And how much I need to cut out of you for it to take."

The first Sauren Gin ever killed was a Jah-Wai, only a cycle

JOSHUA ANDERLE & MICHAEL ANDERLE

from his trial. Raza never forgot that recording and Gin never forgot the Sauren. At least a dozen were felled by him in the cycles since. Some had hunted him for his bounty and others to avenge the fallen as Raza would do now.

"I'm on my way. I will help him in his hunt," he proclaimed.

"I'll send you his tracker signal. He asked that you only notify him when you're half a click away. He's trying to stay dark. My partner has said that another person will join you—a bounty hunter—but he seems to be further out."

"I hope to leave nothing for him," Raza said and signed off. He activated the ship's thrusters and set a course to Wolfson's coordinates. He would show this killer why the Sauren were known as the greatest hunters.

AUTHOR NOTES - MICHAEL

THANK YOU for not only reading this story but these *Author Notes* as well.

(I think I've been good with always opening with "thank you." If not, I need to edit the other *Author Notes*!)

WOOHOO! I've just 'released' a version of the new Bethany Anne story's cover (*Finish What You Started*), and I'm excited we are getting close to releasing this story... Yes, I know it has been a while, but please be patient with me. I'm working on having them come out a bit quicker...

For those who know about stuff I'm planning or working on, please remind me. I think I've lost my mind in the last few days. LOL - <<< (EDIT: He's joking....) (EDIT of the EDIT: No I'm not.) *(Editor's Note: No, he's not)*

I've been talking to Joshua, and we have book 07 on track for a slightly quicker release, I think. This will be Year 03, and the beginning of a new path for our stories.

Because eventually the students grow up and have to leave the comfort of the Animus.

It gets a bit wild out there, folks.

FAN'S NOTES - Where a fan helps me out with THEIR love of reading, and we learn a bit more about our fellow readers out here as I comment occasionally.

Tandra from Melbourne, FL (seriously, I thought it was going to be Australia…)

About how many books do you read a year, or total in your lifetime?

100 or more a year. (I was probably in the 80 to 100 range before I started writing - mostly due to family obligations… If my wife was out of town, it was easily a 4-6 book weekend… Ah, good times!)

Name your favorite LMBPN Series or Character(s) and what you like about them.

Bethany Anne, she is awesome she kicks butt and always is about family. (And Coke - don't forget the Coke ;-))

If you made up an LMBPN Character, what would be three attributes you would use? (For Example, Bethany Anne is Justice, Family (including friends), and Coca Cola. Brownstone is Keeping it Simple - Respect - and BBQ)

Family, Protection of animals, Home cooking. (I'd be curious about what type of cooking? I'm from Texas, so home cooking uses a lot of oil, beef, chicken, gravy, potatoes… Well, that's the central Texas part of my background.)

Tell us a few short sentences about yourself, and your reading hobby (When did you start reading, why, how much do you read and preferred genre's etc. (as ideas)):

I started reading as a 10-year-old to "Deal with my parents' divorce". I am always reading if I'm not gaming or cooking. My family thinks I would rather read than talk to people. (MIKE EDIT: I often would. Sorry, it's more to do with me sucking at conversation and hating to figure it out. Much easier to read than try to talk at times.) I'm all over the map when it comes to the genre of books I read (though the old school romance is off the table now). I think my favorite right now is Supernatural and Paranormal along with futuristic.

You can have my <what?> before you can have my reading time.

I would say food first then maybe my hubby (Damn, Hubby AFTER food so GO HUBBY!)

Place you have loved to read the most in your life - best memories (mine was as a teenager at my grandparents' house under the feather bed on cold days.)

The big shade tree at my grandmother's house. (Spot on...)

AROUND THE WORLD IN 80 DAYS

One of the interesting (at least to me) aspects of my life is the ability to work from anywhere and at any time. In the future, I hope to re-read my own *Author Notes* and remember my life as a diary entry.

WHERE AM I?

Hanging at Aria's FIVE50 eating some pizza while the overtime hockey game (Stanley cup) is going on. Carolina vs. Washington, tied 3 to 3 at the moment. Large group party put on by NISSAN / INFINITI is hanging out here in the back.

Huh, I just noticed they have a buffet table of food back there...

(Editor's note: We've lost Michael, folks!)

FAN PRICING

$0.99 Saturdays (new LMBPN stuff) and $0.99 Wednesday (both LMBPN books and friends of LMBPN books.) Get great stuff from us and others at tantalizing prices.

Go ahead. I bet you can't read just one.

Sign up here: http://lmbpn.com/email/.

HOW TO MARKET FOR BOOKS YOU LOVE

Review them so others have your thoughts, and tell friends and the dogs of your enemies (because who wants to talk to enemies?)... *Enough said ;-)*

Ad Aeternitatem,

Michael Anderle

44940211R00176

Printed in Poland
by Amazon Fulfillment
Poland Sp. z o.o., Wrocław